DORIAN ROCKWOOD

THE MEPHISTO SWAMP MYSTERY

THE MEPHISTO SWAMP MYSTERY

Copyright © 2026 by Dorian Rockwood.

For information contact:

Insundry Productions Books, Gardnerville NV 89460

insundryproductions.com

Cover illustration by Duy Phan

ISBN (ebook): 978-1-962056-15-1

ISBN (paperback): 978-1-962056-16-8

ISBN (hardcover): 978-1-962056-17-5

Library of Congress Control Number: 2025922516

Also By Dorian Rockwood
Treachery Unmasked

The Case Twins Adventures:
The Cash Cache Mystery
The Silent Witness Mystery
The Dungeon of Peril Mystery
The Mephisto Swamp Mystery

Chapter One

The pungent odor of sweat and leather filled the air as Dan and Paul Case entered the Belmont YMCA gym. The metallic clangs coming from the small weight room echoed through the space, competing with the rhythmic thuds of basketballs on the hardwood floor. The brothers made their way to a corner of the large room that housed the boxing program.

Waiting by the ring was Detective Steve Barton. The powerfully built man was young — in his thirties — with black hair and intelligent eyes. He broke into a grin when he saw Dan and Paul approach.

"Hi, guys! Thanks for sparing with me, Paul. But I warn you, I haven't boxed since when I was in the Navy," he said.

"Don't worry. I'll go easy on you." A cocky grin spread across Paul's face.

Paul and Steve stood side by side, reaching their arms toward the sky, twisting their torsos, and bending their legs in a series of stretches. Meanwhile, Dan knelt by the duffel bag, pulling out gloves, tape, a water bottle, and the most important piece of gear to him, his camera.

Warm-ups complete, Steve peeled off his sweatshirt, revealing a muscular torso. Dan noticed the scars that crisscrossed it. He wondered whether those marks were from his days as a cop walking the beat or souvenirs from the battles he fought during the war.

Paul tugged his shirt off over his head, showing a frame that was lean and defined. Although the brothers were well-built, they certainly lacked the bulk of Steve's physique. Paul removed his glasses and laid them atop his shirt, folded at the edge of the ring, making sure they were safely out of the way.

Steve climbed through the ropes and started to wrap his hands. Dan followed him, helping him put on the old leather gloves. Steve gave a nod of thanks before Dan went back to his twin.

"He's built like a brick outhouse." Dan jerked his head toward Steve while he waited for Paul to wrap his hands.

"What am I? Chopped liver?" Paul shot back.

Dan threw a glance at the detective as he helped Paul with his gloves. "Well, not yet." He continued in an innocent voice. "Just thought you'd want to know, my dear brother. You don't want to show up at our high school graduation next week with a black eye or a busted nose, do you?"

"Hardy-har-har," Paul replied.

Dan shrugged. "Of course, it'll be easier to tell who is who that way."

The brothers were identical twins, each six feet tall with brown hair and eyes. The only way most people told them apart was by Paul's glasses and the fact that he was left-handed.

Paul rolled his eyes. "Anyway, in the boxing game, my dear brother, technique is more important than brute strength."

Dan's glance darted between the two fighters, his artist's eye capturing every detail. Steve's muscular frame glistened under the harsh gym lights. "If you say so, slugger. You know, that'll be a great caption for the photo I'll take of you lying flat on your back." He displayed the title in the air with his hands. "'Technique Outweighs Strength.'"

Paul gave Dan a sour look. He flexed his fingers inside the gloves, his face set in the determined expression he always had before a match. "It may just be the other way around, buddy. Just keep your eye on that timer while you take your pretty pictures, Rembrandt."

As Paul strutted to his corner, Dan couldn't help but grin at his brother's bravado. He picked up his camera, making sure the settings were correct. At an irritated "come on, already" from Paul, Dan made his way to the bell, carefully putting down the camera. He fished a stopwatch out of his pocket.

"Alright, gentlemen — and I use the term loosely — touch them up! Let's see what you've got!" Dan called. Paul and Steve moved to the center of the ring and tapped their gloves. "Box!" He yanked the cord on the bell and clicked the stopwatch.

The two fighters stepped forward, each sizing up the other. The sharp crack of leather gloves mixed with the rhythmic sound of their grunts that escaped with every exertion. Their feet shuffled and pivoted over the canvas floor, an ebb and flow of anticipation and strategy, as they exchanged tentative jabs, testing the other. The boxers bobbed and weaved, their movements smooth and precise, as they launched a flurry of quick punches followed by powerful blows. The ropes vibrated with tension as they circled each other, eyes vigilant, both waiting for that perfect split-second opportunity to deliver a decisive strike.

Dan grabbed some photos of the action, his eyes constantly flicking down to the stopwatch. "Thirty seconds!" He put down his camera and stood by the bell, one eye on the watch's ticking second hand. He tugged the rope, sounding the bell. "One-minute rest before round two."

Paul and Steve retreated to their corners while Dan moved quickly between them, offering sips of water from a metal canteen. He then hurried back to the bell, its clang signaling the second round of the sparring session. By the close of the third and final round, the fighters' bodies shone with sweat, their chests heaving with deep breaths. They tapped their gloves again.

"You've got good technique, Paul," Steve gasped as he caught his breath. "Excellent strategy."

Paul wiped the perspiration from his forehead with one forearm. "Thanks. I can't believe you haven't been in the ring for years."

"It's true." Steve laughed. "But I placed third in the 1944 Fleet Championship in the Navy. South Pacific region."

"You never told me that!" Paul sputtered.

"That was five years ago, and I haven't been in the ring in the meantime. Just like I said." Steve grinned. "After we shower, why don't we all go out for burgers?"

"That's for me. I am starving," Paul tapped himself on his chest. "This one's on me, guys."

"What? *You're* paying?" Dan turned to Steve and jerked a thumb toward his sibling. "You hit him once too often in the head."

***

The aroma of sizzling hamburgers and fries wafted through the open cab of the twins' war-surplus jeep as they pulled into the drive-in. The place was bustling with other teenagers. Their laughter and chatter competed with the *Good Rockin' Tonight* tune blaring from the jukebox. The neon lights of the sign reflected off the shiny paint jobs of cars and hot rods parked around the lot.

Dan and Paul jumped up from their seats. A sleek, dark green MG sports car zipped into the parking space beside them, and Steve climbed out. The three strolled over to the window. After they gave their order, Paul slapped down a crisp, new bill on the counter. The clerk, a young teen with a spattering of acne across his cheeks and a voice that wavered like a reed in the wind, glanced at the money. His smile disappeared as his eyes scrutinized it, a hint of uncertainty creeping in.

"I'm, uh, sorry, sir. I can't accept this," he said, sliding the cash back with as much care as if it were a loaded gun about to go off. "It's courntro... cantro... It's fake."

Paul's jaw dropped. "What? Get outta here!"

"We've got flyers about them." The clerk tapped a piece of paper taped to the register to prove it. "The Feds came by today."

Steve stepped forward. "That's okay. I've got this, Paul," he said, pulling out his wallet.

Paul scrutinized the rejected money, holding it up to the light. "It looks fine to me."

"Here, let me take a look." Dan plucked cash from his brother's fingers. "Working as a soda jerk has its perks — like handling cash all day. And all the free soda you can drink." He rubbed the bill between his thumb and forefinger, then nodded. "Yeah, it's definitely off. The paper feels... wrong."

"Huh?" Paul took the bill and felt it.

"There's been a surge of funny money in the area lately. Treasury agents are sniffing around," Steve said to Paul. "Do you recall where you got it?"

Paul's brow furrowed, then he shook his head. "It came from where I keep all my earnings before I deposit them at the bank. My customers usually pay in cash." Paul's mind raced through his landscaping service client list. "Maybe it could be...?" He shrugged. "I don't... I can't remember where I got this specific bill."

Dan nudged Steve. "He's too busy crafting the perfect hedge or planting a pretty petunia to worry about things like that."

Paul handed the money to Dan. "Here. You can use it as a bookmark for all the mysteries you read."

The trio picked up their food and found seats at a nearby table. They sat and started to munch on their burgers. Steve cleared his throat, folding his hands in front of him. "Listen, fellas, there's something I want to discuss with you."

Dan's stomach clenched. He glanced at Paul, who'd paused mid-chew.

"It's about your mother." Steve's voice was uncharacteristically hesitant. "We've been... well, I've taken her out to dinner. A few times."

"Weekly," the twins chorused in perfect unison.

Dan couldn't help adding, "But who's paying attention?"

Steve blinked momentarily, thrown off balance. Then a chuckle escaped him, breaking the tension. "Right. I should've known you two would keep track. Boys, I know how you feel about your dad. I just... I want to make sure you're comfortable with this. With your mom and me seeing each other."

The brothers exchanged glances. Finally, Dan spoke up. "We know Mom deserves to be happy... we want her to be happy. It's just..." He fumbled for words, then shrugged. "I don't know how to explain how we feel about the whole thing."

Steve nodded, understanding in his gaze. "I get it. I'm not trying to replace your dad. There's no way I could. I just... well, hope I can earn a place in your family, if it goes that far. That you will give me a chance."

Dan felt a mix of emotions swirling inside him — grief for his dad, uncertainty, and a respect for Steve's honesty. He looked at Paul, seeing his own conflicted feelings mirrored in his twin's face.

"Thanks for being on the level with us," Dan said after a few moments. "Of course we will."

Paul agreed with a nod, then cracked a grin. "Just don't expect us to start calling you 'Dad' anytime soon."

"Fair enough." Steve's shoulders relaxed visibly. He laughed. "That means a lot to me, boys. I know I've got my work cut out for me, but I'm up for the challenge. Now, how about we tackle these milkshakes before they melt?" Steve wiped a dollop of ketchup from his chin. "So, tell me about this camping trip you've got coming up. Sounds like quite the adventure."

Paul's eyes lit up. "Oh man, Steve, you have no idea. We're going to canoe down the Makatawa to where it meets the Kolbalt River!"

"Maybe even explore some of the Mephisto Swamp!" Dan said.

"Ah, yes, my artistic brother," Paul said, a smile playing at the corners of his mouth. He put on a very bad posh accent and flung his hands in the air to act out his next sentence. "He has decided he simply *must* make sketches for a *divine* landscape painting of the swamp he's been just ever so *dying* to do."

Steve's brow furrowed slightly. "The Mephisto Swamp, huh? Boys, I don't want to be a killjoy, but that area can be treacherous. You sure you know what you're getting into?"

Paul waved away the concern. "No need to be concerned. We've got maps, compasses, the works." He nodded toward his brother. "Daniel Boone here has all but memorized the guidebooks. We're not exactly heading into the wilds of uncharted territory."

Steve held up his hands in mock surrender. "Alright, alright. I can see you've got it all figured out. Just... be careful out there, okay? Your mother would have my head if anything happened to you two. I mean, even if I'm not officially a member of the family."

Paul grinned with a mischievous glint in his eye. "Don't worry, Detective Barton. We won't become your next case."

Dan couldn't help but laugh at the expression on Steve's face — a mix of exasperation and reluctant amusement.

***

Dan stood behind the gleaming counter at the Allen Drugstore, wiping down the marble surface with his usual efficiency coming from years of practice. The familiar clink of the metal cups and sundae dishes filled the air as he next arranged them in neat stacks. The afternoon shift had been slow, with only a few people stopping by for treats or lunch.

He looked up to see his brother saunter in, holding hands with his girlfriend, Betty. Donna was with them. Even though Dan had been going out with Donna for months, he still couldn't believe the prettiest girl in school went for him. Paul caught Dan's eye and waved.

"Hey, soda jerk!" Paul called out, emphasizing the last word. "Your favorite customers have arrived."

"At least two of them have," Dan shot back as the group settled in at one of the small tables. Draping a towel over one arm like he'd seen waiters in a fancy restaurant do in the movies, he approached the table. He spoke with a lousy French accent. "Bonjour, madame and monsieur. What can I bring you all?"

Betty thought for a moment. "I'd like some champagne." Donna nodded in agreement.

Dan spread his hands. "I regret, madame, but we are fresh out. The tap is dry."

"Oh." Donna put on a disappointed expression. She brightened. "How about some caviar, then?"

"Oh, I am so sorry, but the fish, she lay no eggs today." Dan gave a head shake of regret.

Paul held up three fingers. "Then I guess make it cherry cokes all around, garrison."

"Garçon," Betty and Donna corrected in unison.

"That, too," Paul returned.

"An excellent choice, monsieur. We have a fine vintage." Dan kissed his fingertips and went back to the soda fountain to make the drinks. He served them to Paul, Donna and Betty with a flourish. "That will be..." He pretended to count on his fingers. "That will be thirty cents."

Paul dug into his pocket and handed some change to Dan. Dan examined the coins suspiciously and bit the quarter. Paul groaned. "They're real, dunderhead."

"Forgive moi, monsieur. But you seem... what is the word?" Dan tapped his temple as he tried to remember. "Ah, yes! Shady! You seem shady."

The girls giggled. "He knows you!" Betty said to Paul.

"Oh, waiter!" Donna crooked her finger. Dan went over to her and leaned down. She kissed him. "That is your tip, handsome."

As usual, Dan blushed when Donna called him that. Paul laughed.

"Tell him that again, Donna," Paul encouraged. "Go on. I want to see if we can make him glow like a beet."

Dan mustered his dignity and stood tall. He jerked a thumb over his shoulder. "Monsieur, the guillotine is waiting for you in the alley. Your head... you will not miss it."

An elderly lady entered the soda fountain and headed for a stool.

"Pardon moi. A regular." Dan bowed and went back to the counter. He dropped the accent. "Afternoon, Miss Tibbs."

"Good afternoon, Dan," Miss Tibbs said as she got comfortable on the stool.

"The usual?" Dan asked. "BLT with extra mayo, and a cup of tea?"

"Yes, that's it." Miss Tibbs looked around, then asked almost shyly. "And Dan, could I have two Ry-Krisp crackers today?"

"Of course!" Dan smiled. "I could make it three, if you want."

Miss Tibbs shook her head. "Oh, no! I'm watching my weight."

"I understand. Your sandwich will be right up." Dan set to work preparing the food.

He had just set the sandwich, a steaming cup of tea, and two Ry-Krisps in front of Miss Tibbs when he heard squeals coming from Betty and Donna.

"Ricardo!"

Dan wheeled toward the sound. Standing by the table was Ricardo Romero, the Treasury Department agent the brothers met during their last adventure. His movie-star handsome face broke into a smile as he spotted the twins. Donna and Betty had already gotten to their feet to greet him, flanking him on either side like eager bookends.

"Ladies, you're making me blush," Ricardo said, his voice carrying that hint of a Spanish accent that seemed to make the girls swoon even more.

Donna had linked her arm through his right elbow while Betty mirrored the pose on his left. Their faces glowed with excitement as they escorted him toward their table. Ricardo's dark eyes scanned the room with that piercing gaze of his, taking in every detail despite his casual demeanor.

"Ricardo," Paul called out, rising from his seat. He shook hands. "What brings the Treasury's finest to our little town?"

Ricardo extricated himself from Donna and Betty with gentle politeness. "Just passing through. Heard this place makes the best milkshakes in three counties."

Dan raised an eyebrow. Treasury agents didn't just "pass through" small towns like Farmingford for milkshakes. He wiped his hands on his apron. "Be right back," he said to Miss Tibbs, then headed toward the growing commotion.

"Is it about that counterfeit?" Dan asked as he shook hands with Ricardo.

Ricardo's eyes flashed with interest. "What's that about counterfeit, Dan?"

"I got paid with funny money and tried to use it." Paul relayed what had happened at the burger stand.

"Do you still have it?" the Treasury agent asked.

"My dear brother palmed it off on me. I think it's still in my wallet." Dan fished out the counterfeit and handed it to Ricardo.

Ricardo gave a slight nod, his face impassive, as he examined the bill. He pulled a small notebook from his jacket and opened it with a flick of his wrist. His eyes moved between the bill and the page multiple times. "Can I keep this?"

"Sure," both twins said together.

"It's an example of the counterfeits we're tracking down. The serial numbers match." Ricardo slipped the bill into the pages of his notebook and then tucked it back into his pocket.

"Ah, remember our fingerprints are on it," Dan said nervously. He gestured to himself and his brother. "And… ah… we're not involved."

Ricardo laughed. "Don't worry, Dan. It's very difficult to get prints off a bill, and it's rarely successful if it's tried. The paper is porous. Any prints are smudged, overlapped, or just worn off."

Dan grinned. "That's a relief."

"Are they well-done counterfeits, Ricardo?" Betty asked.

"They are excellent," Ricardo answered. "Created by a master."

"Except for the paper," Paul put in. "It feels wrong."

"That's a smart observation, Paul," Betty said.

"It is. Most people would miss that," Ricardo said with an approving nod.

Paul gave a modest shrug. Dan gave him a dirty look.

"So these fakes are being passed around here?" Donna asked.

Ricardo shook his head. "A few, but they have been popping up all over the country. A sizeable batch recently appeared in Davenport, so we're scouring the tri-state area. That narrows down the search."

"Three states? That's narrower?" Dan asked.

Ricardo laughed. "Narrower than the entire continental United States. The gang may be headquartered in the region. I'm talking to banks and businesses in this area. But let's forget my job for a moment."

"Let's." Donna took a step toward Ricardo. "So now tell us all about your wedding!"

"And don't you dare leave anything out!" Betty said.

Dan excused himself and returned to Miss Tibbs. She had just finished her sandwich and was daintily dabbing her mouth with a napkin.

"Everything okay?" Dan asked with a smile.

"Tasty as usual, Dan," Miss Tibbs answered. She dug around in her purse. "I only have a ten-dollar bill." She pulled one out.

"That's fine." Dan took it and hesitated. The paper felt wrong... the bill was another counterfeit.

"Is something the matter, Dan?" Miss Tibbs asked.

"No, nothing. Let me get you your change." Dan went to the register and made change, counting it back to Miss Tibbs.

"And this is for you, Dan." Miss Tibbs gave him two quarters.

"Thank you," Dan said.

After Miss Tibbs stepped away from the counter, Dan took out his wallet. He pulled out the money for Mrs. Tibb's tab, placed it into the cash drawer, and then rejoined the others.

"That sounded so romantic!" Donna gushed.

"A honeymoon in Hawaii!" Betty said.

Paul was attempting not to look too bored during the whole wedding discussion. He wasn't doing very well.

Dan handed the ten-dollar bill to Ricardo. "Here's another one for your collection."

Ricardo's face resumed a businesslike expression as he took it. "Do you know who the passer was?"

Dan nodded in the direction of Miss Tibbs, now browsing the latest romance magazines at the newsstand. "Not exactly the picture of a hardened counterfeiter, is she?"

Ricardo laughed. "No. Well, I have an appointment with the bank manager. It was great to see you all again."

After a round of goodbyes, Ricardo left. Betty and Donna faced the brothers.

"You two aren't going to get involved with this counterfeit stuff, are you?" Betty folded her arms, nailing the brothers with an accusatory look. Donna copied the pose.

"Like you did with that missing gang loot?" Donna asked.

"Or the protection arson ring?" Betty went on.

"Or the kidnapping of the Maitland heir?" Donna finished up.

"Us? No! No!" Paul protested, hands up in surrender.

"We're not going anywhere near funny money or counterfeiters!" Dan sliced his hand through the air to chop off such a thought.

"All we're going to do is take a canoe camping trip," Paul added. "In the middle of nowhere."

"And you can take that," Dan slapped his hand against the table for emphasis, "to the bank!"

Chapter Two

As the dawning sun peeked over the horizon, the used 1942 Studebaker truck came to a halt at Makatawa River Resort, sending a plume of dust into the air. Despite its worn look, it still ran as if it were brand new, even after seven years and unknown miles not clocked by the broken odometer. Paul had bought the vehicle a few months ago, which now proudly bore "Case Landscaping Services" on its sides, painted by Dan, marking the start of Paul's post-graduation business venture.

"Ready for the adventure of a lifetime?" Paul said, slapping Dan's shoulder.

Dan grinned, pushing open the creaky door. "Ready to challenge the wilderness, my dear brother and fellow alumnus of Farmingford High School."

They hopped out of the truck. Though the temperature had not yet climbed, they were prepared for the sweltering heat that was forecast for later in the day. The twins wore matching outfits for a change: crisp white t-shirts, navy blue swimsuits, and well-worn sneakers.

Behind them, their mother's car rolled to a stop, the engine purring softly before it was silenced. She stepped out, sunglasses perched on her head, followed by Steve. He stretched as he climbed out, casting a glance at the clear sky.

"Last chance to back out, guys," Steve said as he and Mrs. Case walked toward the truck.

"Give up. You don't have a prayer, Steve," Mrs. Case said. She was an attractive woman in her mid-thirties, equipped with an unexpected toughness, which served her when she had to go toe-to-toe with city council members or meter readers as the first woman county water department manager. "Tony and the boys planned this trip for when they graduated, after he got back…" Her voice trailed off, her eyes became misty.

Dan was all too familiar with how the sentence would usually end: "got back from the war." Yet, a constant weight sat in his heart, as their father didn't return, never making it off Omaha Beach on D-Day alive. The memory seemed to hang in the air, both a source of honor to him and his brother, but also an ache that never fully healed.

After a moment of quiet, Mrs. Case looked at the twins with a mixture of pride and sadness. "He'd be so proud of you two. Just as I am." She moved closer and wrapped the two in a tight embrace. A lump rose in Dan's throat, and he was caught off guard by the unexpected rush of emotion. As they pulled apart, he felt comforted and anxious at the same time. "Just promise me you'll be careful, boys."

"We always are, Mom," Dan reassured her.

"We're not looking for any trouble," Paul said.

Mrs. Case flashed a knowing smile. "I know, but it always seems to find you. Sometimes, I think you two are magnets."

"Ah, Mom. We'll be in the middle of a swamp or a river." Paul adjusted his glasses. "Nothing can get us there. Except drowning. Or maybe an alligator."

"No alligators up here," Dan reminded his twin.

Steve cleared his throat and spoke in a serious tone. "Listen, fellas, that swamp can be treacherous. Make sure you stick to your maps and don't take any unnecessary risks."

Paul grinned. "Aw, come on, Steve. You're talking to the Case twins here. We eat unnecessary risks for breakfast."

Dan gave a concerned glance toward their mother, then delivered a warning elbow to his brother. "What Paul means is, we'll watch our step."

"Of course we will." Paul quickly turned back to the truck. He dropped open the tailgate and started untying the ropes holding their cedar canoe. "Alright, Dan, let's get this beauty unloaded."

The brothers lifted the canoe onto their shoulders and made their way through the dirt to the water's edge. Once there, they placed it down, watching it float gently on the ripples. Mrs. Case and Steve soon joined them, arms full of camping gear wrapped in waterproof covers. Together, they packed the tent, sleeping bags, and food supplies into the canoe. Paul knelt next to it, carefully arranging everything to balance the weight evenly. After ensuring everything was in place, he stood up, brushed the sand from his hands, and looked over their work with a pleased smile. He stepped back, admiring the fully loaded canoe, ready for their adventure.

"The wilderness calls." Paul handed Dan an oar. He turned to Steve. "Thanks for driving my truck back home. The key is in the ignition."

"You bet," Steve said. "Don't forget to signal if you need help!"

"Sure thing, Steve," Dan replied with a grin. "We packed both carrier pigeons and a flare gun."

Mrs. Case hugged each brother again. "Have fun, boys."

"Thanks, Mom," the twins said as one.

"We'll call you in three days, when we paddle into the Kobalt River Marina," Paul said.

"All grizzled-looking and dirty," Dan added.

"And probably smelly, too," Paul put in.

"If that's the case, I'll bring the truck, and you two will ride home back in the bed," Mrs. Case said.

The twins carefully stepped into the canoe, the wooden frame creaking slightly under their shared weight. Dan settled himself at the back while his brother sat at the front. They each took hold of an oar and pushed off from the riverbank, creating ripples in the water around the canoe. As they drifted into the open river, their mom and Steve remained on the shore, waving goodbye.

The brothers responded with a final, enthusiastic wave before dipping their oars into the cool, clear water and starting their synchronized paddling. They glanced back at the shore again as Mrs. Case got into the family car, while Steve climbed into Paul's truck.

"Dan, do you think Mom is serious about Steve?" Paul asked.

"I've been thinking about that, my dear brother," Dan answered. "The way I figure it, if Mom tells him about her and Dad's past, then we know she's serious."

Mrs. Case recently told the brothers that during their teenage years, they were part of Lorenzo Rizzo's bootlegging gang in Chicago during Prohibition. Their mother stressed that they steered clear of any "nasty business." When their father survived an assault on Rizzo's gang by a rival, their parents decided to leave it all behind, elope, and start new as a family in the small town of Farmingford. Although she insisted she wasn't embarrassed by her background, the family chose not to spread the story around, either.

"I'll buy that," Paul said. "Then the ball would be in Steve's court. He'll have to react to it."

"It would be interesting to see," Dan said. "How would a detective deal with dating a woman who used to be in a bootlegger's gang?"

The Makatawa River stretched wide at this point, but not very deep, its surface shimmering under the early morning sun. Scattered across the water, a handful of rowboats bobbed, each cradling one or two fishermen, their silhouettes framed by broad-brimmed hats and the arc of their fishing rods. Paul and Dan paddled in unison, their canoe gliding through the river, slicing cleanly through the gentle ripples. The current guided them farther from the resort's tidy outpost, drawing them deeper into the wilderness.

"I'm glad we started out when we did. It was a couple of hours to get here," Paul said. "That gives us a good fifteen hours of daylight."

"You weren't that glad earlier," Dan chided. "It took Mom and me pulling you out of bed by your ankles."

"Who knew three o'clock in the morning came so early?" Paul protested.

As the river made a graceful curve around a bend, the dense, packed woods pressed right up against its banks, their leafy branches nearly brushing the water's surface. Dan took a deep breath, filling his lungs with the rich, earthy aroma of the forest — a blend of damp soil, decaying leaves, and the fresh, invigorating scent of pine needles mingling in the crisp air.

"Man, this is the life," Dan said, his voice barely above a whisper as he let the atmosphere soak in. "Just us, nature, and endless possibilities."

"It's beautiful, but keep paddling, buddy," Paul replied. He started to chant like a coxswain. "Stroke! Stroke! Stroke!"

"You mean like this?" Dan flipped his oar backward to splash Paul.

With a mischievous grin on his face, Paul retaliated, hurling a splash of water back at his brother. Dan gave a playful scowl and returned fire. Both brothers soon engaged in a full-scale battle, laughing, until they were soaked through.

"Okay, okay! Peace! Peace!" Paul set down his paddle and raised his hands in surrender. Although it was still early morning, the sun beat down, its heat amplified by the humidity. "I'm shucking my shirt, so I can dry off. Ah, I think I'll just leave it off. It's going to be hot today, anyway. And we don't have to act civilized or anything out here."

"You're right. We're just a couple of wild guys." Dan hated wearing wet clothes, so he stripped to the waist. He twisted toward his brother, pounded his chest, and pointed to himself. "Me, Tarzan."

Paul repeated the gesture, then aimed his index finger at Dan. "You, dope." As he tugged his t-shirt over his head, the canoe wobbled, threatening to capsize them. Dan gripped the sides, steadying their craft.

"Careful, you big oaf!" Dan yelped. "You're tipping us over!"

"Take it easy, I've got this under con —" Paul's words were cut short as his glasses caught on his shirt, flying off his face and disappearing over the side of the canoe with a soft 'plop'.

"Oh, for crying out loud," Paul groaned, squinting at the ripples. "Mom's gonna kill me."

Dan couldn't help but laugh. "Now who's the dope, dope?" He imitated a movie gangster. "Your specs are now sleeping with the fishes, bub."

Paul ran a hand through his brown hair, a mix of frustration and amusement on his face. "Well, I guess I'll be relying on my dear brother for this trip if we have to read anything."

They paddled on, their oars slicing through the water in a steady rhythm. Bit by bit, the landscape to their right changed, with the river expanding until the line between land and river vanished.

Tall cypress and tupelo trees emerged from the calm, dark waters, their enormous trunks widening at the base. The bald cypress knees jutted out from the surface like silent sentinels, their surfaces polished by hundreds of years and the soft caress of wind and rain, standing as evidence of the buffing effects of the elements. Their branches stretched outward.

The brothers stowed their oars inside the boat and gazed at the landscape surrounding them. Dense greenery and twisted branches formed a natural barrier along the water's edge. Suddenly, as if responding to an unseen signal, a flock of birds burst from the leaves, their wings flapping wildly as they filled the sky with sharp, echoing cries. The twins turned to each other, their eyes alive with a mix of curiosity and awe.

"This must be the place. Mephisto Swamp." Dan looked around and gave a low whistle. "Wow. It looks like somewhere in Louisiana. It's like a Viavant painting."

"Who?"

"George Louis Viavant," Dan said, "was a New Orleans painter known for his bayou and swamp landscapes."

"That's my dear brother," Paul gave a chuckle. "Can name artists off the top of his head, but has no idea who pitches for the Cubs."

"Johnny Schmitz," Dan smirked over his shoulder at Paul.

Paul spread his arms and bowed at the waist. "I am humbled." He sat up and gazed at the tangle of trees. "Mephisto Swamp... Devil Swamp. It's well-named."

Dan nodded. "It sure is. You can imagine Satan living somewhere in all that."

Paul glanced around. "But... ah, no alligators, huh?"

"Not this far north. I told you already," Dan answered.

"Thanks for the reassurance. Well, where's the way in, pathfinder?" Paul waved one hand at the trees. "Didn't you tell me that some kind of marking…"

Dan used one hand to shade his eyes. "Yeah… the water trails are marked by a reflector on the trunks of —" He pointed. "There's one just ahead."

Paul squinted and leaned forward. "I'll have to take your word for it."

For a moment, neither one made a move to start paddling again.

"Nervous?" Dan tried to make it sound like a joke. It fell flat.

Paul returned Dan's look, then squared his shoulders. "Danny boy, remember the two of us have faced down gangsters, arsonists, and kidnappers. What can a spooky old swamp throw at the Case Twins that we can't handle?"

Dan grinned. "Now that you put it that way…"

The brothers leaned forward, their muscles tensing as they plunged the wooden oars into the still, glassy surface of the water. The canoe glided toward the shadowy entrance of the swamp. Twisted trees loomed overhead, their gnarled branches intertwined like skeletal fingers waiting to snatch them up. The air was heavy and humid, filled with a chorus of sounds — frogs croaking in rhythmic bursts, insects buzzing in the dense underbrush, and the occasional splash from a fish jumping out of the water to catch an insect.

Dan's stroke faltered for a moment, the paddle blade leaving a sluggish trail in the wake. It seemed the swampland was waiting. For what, he couldn't say. Perhaps for them?

He peered into the depths of the thick vegetation with a mixture of fascination and unease. There was a beauty here, to be sure, but it was a dark, twisted one that whispered of secrets and dangers lurking just below the surface or hidden in the undergrowth.

"Boy, this place can give you the heebie-jeebies. It's like we've paddled into another world," Paul murmured, his voice uncharacteristically subdued.

Dan only nodded in response. His artist's eye soon overcame his initial disquiet, as he scanned the vibrant scene before him.

The landscape was a blend of shapes and colors, light and shadow playing across the cypress trees, their trunks weathered and majestic. A lush mat of duckweed spread along the water's surface, a living carpet of green that shimmered under the sun. Scattered among them, American lotuses floated along, their leaves broad and a deep, rich green. Some were in full bloom, their creamy yellow blossoms perched atop slender stalks, swaying in the breeze like delicate crowns.

The twins paddled on, gliding through the swamp, intruders in an alien world. Above them, the thick canopy of leaves created a shadowy world of greens and browns, letting only a few rays of sunlight skip and twinkle on the surface. Each time they dipped their paddles, ripples spread out like heralds announcing the arrival of strangers as the canoe moved through the duckweed. The air was filled with a rich, earthy scent — a mix of rotting leaves, wet wood, and the slight sulfuric hint of stagnant water.

"So there aren't any alligators, but something strange could live out here," Paul said.

"Such as?"

"Like in that story I heard." It was clear to Dan that Paul was setting something up.

Dan became a little uncomfortable. While he devoured mystery stories, he wasn't fond of spooky stuff. But he had to ask, "What story?"

Paul leaned forward and spoke in a confidential tone, as if not wanting to be overheard. "Wild-man Wendell."

"Who?" Dan squirmed in his seat. He knew asking his brother not to tell him anymore would be an invitation to constant ribbing. Better to let Paul get it out of his system.

"Wild-man Wendell." Paul went on in a melodramatic voice, like the announcer on a scary radio show. "He was some loony old coot who lived out here... chased out of normal civilization, because normal civilization wouldn't have him. He claimed all this swampland was his alone. And he guarded it. He'd bury his bloody hatchet deep into the cranium of anybody who dared set foot in his domain."

"Paul..." Dan groaned.

His twin continued, obviously relishing the tale. "And he'd drag them back to his camp. He'd skin their bodies, sometimes while his writhing victims were still alive. Screaming! He'd boil them in an iron pot with some carrots and turnips, maybe a dash of oregano and a pinch of salt... then eat them!" He smacked his lips. "Yummy! Yummy! Yummy! To this very day, people tell stories of Wild-man Wendell's demonic ghost, with blazing eyes of fire, haunting the swamp, still ready to protect his land from all trespassers!" Paul gave a chilling laugh.

Dan faced his brother. "I'm going to pitch you overboard so the gators can eat you."

"You said there were no alligators out here." Paul nervously checked the water around the canoe.

"I lied." Dan flashed a sweet smile.

"So did I. There wasn't any Wild-man Wendell." Paul paused a second. "His name was really Crazy Chester." He drew out the word "crazy."

Dan rolled his eyes and turned his focus back to the captivating show of light and shadow. The waterway expanded, exposing a patch of dry earth that appeared to be resisting the advancing swamp. This piece of land was filled with tall trees and dense underbrush, its vivid greens contrasting with the sluggish water the brothers had traveled through. The air buzzed with the sounds of hidden creatures, creating a lively sanctuary in the midst of the wetlands.

"Look... those poles sticking up over there, next to the land," Paul pointed. "They almost could be an old dock."

Two lines of weathered posts, decayed and crumbling, poked out from the murky swamp. The wood was mottled with patches of moss and algae. The water lapping at the bases was a dark greenish-brown, swirling gently with the occasional ripple.

"They could be," Dan said. "The guidebooks said that back in the early 1900s, sawmills were set up around the swamp to harvest the cypress. If some lumbering work was going on in this area, it makes sense they'd need a dock."

"Of course, it could have belonged to Crazy Chester," Paul hinted. "He's waiting for us just beyond those trees…"

"Oh, shut up," Dan replied. "You're safe in any case. Any axe of his would bounce off your thick skull." He checked the rotted poles again. "Let's pull in and take a break. We don't know when we'll spot dry land again. And we've got plenty of time. It's still early. We can tie off at that post nearest the shore."

They steered toward the tilting remains of the dock, their canoe scraping softly against the muddy shore as they landed.

Chapter Three

Before Dan finished tying off the canoe to a post, Paul scrambled out. He stood on the dry land, feet shoulder-width apart and fists on hips. The conqueror.

"I claim this land in the name of Paul and Dan Case," he proclaimed.

Dan followed his brother ashore. "No, no, my dear brother. You have that backwards. Dan and Paul Case, you mean."

"How do you figure that?" Paul protested. "The order is simple, bonehead. I should be top billing, since I'm the older brother."

"Older by only two minutes, remember," Dan said. He held up two fingers. "I'm holding up two fingers in case you can't see them."

"Still counts," Paul returned. "And I can see your hand, funny guy. Although it looks like four fingers."

"Besides, it should be in alphabetical order," Dan said. "'D' is before 'P'. You do remember kindergarten, don't you?"

"Like it was yesterday." Paul thought for a moment. "Okay, how about 'I claim this land in the name of the Case Twins?'"

Dan nodded. "That works for me."

Paul struck his pose again. "I claim this land in the name of the Case Twins." He shot a glance at his brother. "Paul and Dan."

Dan rolled his eyes, then the two grinned. They stood side by side for a moment, taking in the sight before them. Their sneakers squelched softly in the mud as they shifted their weight. Together, they stepped onto the dry dirt.

"Let's do a little exploring," Dan suggested with a nod toward the dense woods. "There may be something back there. You know, the building that used this dock. It might make an excellent subject for a painting for me when we get back. I could get some sketches."

"Go ahead, Rembrandt," Paul said as he sprawled out on a wide, flat rock. "I'm going to lie here in the sun like a big, old, lazy cat."

"In other words, business as usual," Dan said.

"In other words, business as usual," Paul mimicked. He dismissed his brother with a wave of his hand. "Just don't wander off." Linking his fingers behind his head, he closed his eyes with a contented sigh. "And watch out for crazed hermits."

Dan's gaze flitted from the gnarled trees to the shadowy underbrush, each mysterious shape and muted color beckoning him deeper into the wild scene. Automatically, the artist in him started picturing different compositions and palettes for paintings. It was too bad his easel and paints were too awkward to pack with them.

"There's what looks like what's left of an old road leading off over there. It must lead somewhere." Dan went back to the canoe and reached in, pulling out his small sketchbook and pencil. "I promise I won't stray from it."

"Okay, but be careful," Paul said without opening his eyes, the words floating through the humid air. "Only don't come crying back to me if Crazy Chester cuts your head off with his rusty axe."

"Don't worry," Dan said. "I wouldn't dream of interrupting your beauty sleep. You certainly need all of it you can get."

Paul stuck one hand in the air and made a talking gesture. "Blah, blah, blah."

Dan headed down the old road. He maneuvered over a tangled root, the ground spongy underfoot, his sneakers leaving faint impressions in the loam. His breath grew shallow as he walked deeper into the woods, the muffled sound of his own footsteps mingling with the forest's hushed tones.

After a while, he stopped and flipped open his pad. With quick, precise strokes, Dan sketched the path as it curved out of sight behind more trees. He could see a painting of this scene using a palette of blues and greens, emphasizing mystery.

As he drew, a metallic clacking pierced the natural chorus — a steady, rhythmic pulse that seemed both near and distant. It sounded like the muted chatter of metal — gears shifting and levers clicking. That blended with the occasional soft creak of well-worn hinges and a gentle but distinct thump, like the measured beat of a slow drum.

Clack-clack-thump. Clack-clack-thump.

Dan tried to figure out where the sound was coming from, but he was sure it didn't come from Mother Nature. It bounced off the trees, hiding its source among the shadows. A prickle of unease crawled up Dan's spine. His eyes darted from one tree to another, half-expecting some hidden creature of the swamp to emerge. Or Crazy Chester.

Then the noise stopped.

The only place the mysterious noise could have come from was beyond the turn of the winding road. He hesitated for a moment, then steeled himself and decided to push forward. The thick air clung to his skin, growing heavier and more oppressive. The humidity wrapped around him like a wet blanket, and beads of sweat began to form on his forehead, trickling down his temples. He rounded the curve.

Dan spotted a structure peeking through the trees. He moved forward and at last emerged into a clearing. In the center stood an unexpectedly large old sawmill. The two-story rectangular building, both imposing and desolate, loomed large, competing with the surrounding trees. Its weathered walls remained defiant against the elements. Iron shutters, their surfaces rusted but solid-looking, sealed the windows. Around twenty feet of ground, still marked by tire tracks and wagon ruts baked in by the sun, separated the building from the forest.

This sawmill must have been an important operation, given how big the structure was. He could make out "Walton Lumber Company" painted in now-faded letters running along the top of the building, just below the roof. It was as if the mill hadn't been abandoned, but secured for future use... which never happened.

He remembered what he had read in the guidebooks. Once, Mephisto Swamp had been home to a thriving logging industry, since cypress was prized for its durability and stability. Men had toiled among these trees, felling them to feed the hungry saws of mills like the one in front of him. He could almost see the ghostly figures of laborers hauling the mighty trunks through the mud, could hear the whine of the blades as they sliced through the tough wood.

His mind's eye instinctively designed a composition for a painting, pushing aside the unsettling sounds he'd heard. He shifted his position, seeking the best angle. Flipping open his sketchbook again, he began to work.

As usual, he slipped into a different frame of mind when he drew. His eyes, brain, and hand merged into a unified flow. Yet, the strange noise gnawed at the edges of his concentration and curiosity. He made himself forget all of that as he continued to work... until the noise came again.

Clack-clack-thump. Clack-clack-thump.

Dan's hand halted, his pencil hovering over the page. It was the same sound. A rhythmic metallic chattering, each beat resonating from deep within the mill's core, as if a mechanical heartbeat.

Clack-clack-thump. Clack-clack-thump.

Intrigued by the sound, he closed his sketchbook. He walked around the building to the back, where a roughly dug canal extended from the swamp to the mill. This channel, now filled with mud and tangled roots, most likely was used to carry cut trees to the saw. The rear of the building was one giant opening, with the vast interior faintly lit by the sun seeping through the wall's cracks. Dan squinted into the dimness and spotted the huge, jagged saw blade in the center, its teeth-edge looking still sharp and intimidating.

He made his way to the distant side of the mill, his sneakers crunching on the dirt. A wide road lay between the structure and another section of forest, but Dan saw flashes of sunlight glinting off water through the trees. He and Paul had ended up on a peninsula, a dry finger of land in the middle of the swamp. At the far end of the building, at the end of the lengthy wooden wall, Dan noticed one shutter hanging open. The strange noise appeared to come from inside there.

Clack-clack-thump. Clack-clack-.

The noise ceased abruptly. Dan froze, his heart racing. Logic screamed at him to retreat, to go back to Paul and the safety of their canoe, and paddle away. If he did drag his twin back here, and the sound was something normal, like a shutter blowing in the wind, Dan would never hear the end of it. He would say Dan reads too many mystery books. Better to just return to the canoe...

Yet his curiosity tugged at him, urging him to investigate further. He inhaled deeply, attempting to steady his nerves, and hesitated a moment before edging toward the open shutter.

Keeping close to the rough wood wall, Dan edged towards the window, the soles of his shoes crunching against the dirt. He skirted a pair of bulkhead basement doors and another closed door until he reached the window. He paused for a second, waiting to see if the sound would repeat itself. It didn't, but some other noises came from inside: rustling, of somebody moving around.

His mind flipped back to the Crazy Chester story and wondered if he was about to find out if Paul's scary tale was true. He shook his head, pushing that idea out of his brain. He leaned forward, drawn by an irresistible urge to see what lay in the interior.

A room extended across the entire width of the mill's end, filled with a few dusty desks and chairs. A layer of dust covered most surfaces, although a few had been wiped clean for use. Windows lined two adjacent walls, forming an L-shape at the building's corner. One window remained closed, but Dan stood by the open one, allowing a soft stream of sunlight to illuminate the space. At one end of the room, there was a sturdy wooden door, partly glazed. A couple of boxes of what looked like blank paper rested in one corner.

In contrast to the dirty surroundings, standing in the center of the room was a gleaming, portable printing press, the kind operated by a foot pedal. Its metal frame glinted under the light coming through the window, highlighting the machine's intricate gears and levers. A young boy, no older than 13 or 14, popped up from behind the machine.

He was short, up to Dan's shoulder, maybe, and of a slight build. A mop of long, black curly hair bounced with each move. In his hand, he held a small oil can, its spout glistening as he carefully lubricated one of the press's joints. As the oil seeped into the mechanism with a smooth, satisfying ease, a grin spread across his face — the pride of tending a well-maintained machine. Just as he was about to place the can down on a nearby shelf, he caught sight of Dan peering in. He jumped and quickly glanced around.

"Hey! What do you think you're doing?" The kid spoke in an urgent whisper. He rushed to the window.

"Uh, just looking," Dan stammered, stepping back from the sill. "I wasn't spying. I heard the noise and —"

"You shouldn't be here," the other boy warned, his voice carrying an undertone that hinted at more than concern — it was fear, raw and unfiltered. His hands trembled slightly as he talked, and the darting movements of his eyes displayed his nervousness, perhaps of being discovered. "You need to leave. Now. Scram. Fast."

"Okay, okay. I'm going." Dan agreed, backing away, his curiosity now tinged with unease. He was wondering what could link together an old mill, a printing press, and the agitated kid before him.

No sooner had the word "going" left his lips than another voice — raspy and harsh — sounded from behind him. "Now that ain't no way to treat a visitor, Mousey."

Dan whipped around, his eyes widening as he faced a towering figure.

The man loomed over him, not bulky with fat or chiseled with muscle, but simply enormous, with a commanding presence that demanded attention. His hair was cropped short, like a wheat field after harvest, and the bridge of his nose bore the evidence of an old injury, crooked and a bit flattened. His sheer size was daunting, and the glint in his squinty eyes suggested he was aware of the intimidation his bulk could wield. He wore a rumpled suit, minus the tie, giving the impression of an unmade bed.

The big man looked Dan over, wearing only a swimsuit and sneakers, and grinned. "Who do we have here? Tarzan? We should invite Tarzan in, Mousey. For a cup of tea." He rumbled a chuckle.

"I need to go." Dan's voice came out more as a plea than a command, his heart thundering against his ribs. He cast a desperate glance toward Mousey, who had taken several steps back. His eyes were wide, offering no help but seemingly a silent apology.

The man whipped a gun out of his pocket and pointed it at Dan. "Nah, I insist." The man grinned, his teeth crooked and tobacco-stained. "Mousey, get the door."

"Yeah, Rocky. Okay, Rocky, sure thing, Rocky," Mousey said, rushing out of the room.

The exterior door next to the window creaked open. Rocky waved his revolver in an unspoken command. Dan stepped through the door into the mill.

He was in a square hallway. Shadows gathered in the corners, tangled like cobwebs. In front of him, three closed doors stood in a row, their surfaces marred by chipped and peeling paint. To his right, the half-glassed door opened to the room holding the printing press, marked by a once-elegant sign, now faded and barely legible, that read "Office". To his left, he suspected the door led to the saw room he'd glimpsed earlier. Metal bars and a sturdy padlock, resembling the forbidding entrance to a prison cell, secured this door.

"Open the right one," Rocky said to Mousey, nodding toward a door.

Mousey scrambled to obey. Rocky prodded Dan in his back with the gun barrel.

Dan walked toward the open doorway. Rocky's heavy boots thudded against the creaky wooden planks beneath him, each step sending an ominous echo reverberating through the hollow, desolate space as he followed.

"Inside," Rocky said, shoving Dan forward. The force pushed him against the far wall. He dropped his sketchbook and pencil in the collision. "You're gonna sit tight and keep your trap shut if you know what's good for ya."

Rocky towered over Dan, the threat in his stance clear and powerful. Dan's gaze flickered to the man's hands — they looked capable of inflicting damage without any difficulty at all — without the use of a weapon.

"Got it, bub?" Rocky snarled, his eyes narrowed slits that bore into Dan's own.

"Y-yes," Dan managed to choke out. Every muscle in his body tensed for an opportunity to escape that didn't come. He didn't know why, but he tacked on: "sir."

"Sir?" Rocky grinned. "Sir?" He laughed. "I like the sound of that." He said the word again as though trying on a fashionable new suit. "Sir!"

With one last glare that silently conveyed dire consequences, Rocky stepped out, slamming the door. A bolt slid across the other side with a decisive click. Dan was alone, his rapid breathing the only company. Voices from the hallway broke the silence.

"What are you going to do with him, Rocky?" Mousey asked.

"Nuttin', at least for now. It's up to the Professor," Rocky's voice hardened. "But what's the idea of openin' up that window?"

"Well, gee, Rocky, it was so hot and stuffy inside," Mousey whined back. "I didn't think it would do no harm."

"That's the problem. You don't think, punk," Rocky fired back.

"How was I to know that guy would be wandering around, huh? I mean, what are the odds, huh? Huh, Rocky?" Mousey gave a weak laugh.

"That's why the Professor gave that order about the windows, you stupid idiot!" Rocky roared. "Only the one on the second floor can be opened! You need to learn to follow instructions!"

"No, Rocky! Please!" Mousey begged.

The nauseating thud of a backhand landing came through the wall, soon accompanied by the noise of a body falling and a cry.

"Get up," Rocky snarled.

"I'm sorry, Rocky, I'm sorry. It'll never happen again. The window, I mean..." Mousey whimpered.

"You bet it won't, shrimp!"

There was the sound of another slap and another yelp.

It was too much for Dan. He ran to the door and pounded on it. "Stop it! Leave him alone!"

"Stow it, you, or I'll give you the same treatment! But I won't be so gentle-like!" Rocky yelled back. "Now, Mousey, get up, and quit your snivellin'. I'll close that damn shutter myself. You go upstairs. Wait for Vic and Tommy to get back."

"Yeah, yeah, sure, Rocky, sure," Mousey said in a trembling voice, "whatever you say."

"Sir!" Rocky bellowed.

"Sir," Mousey said, his tone soft and meek. A door opened and closed, followed by footsteps mounting creaky stairs.

Rocky's laughter faded as he went into the office and shut the door.

Dan's eyes roamed the shadowy room, straining to make out shapes in the semi-darkness. There was no window to let in daylight, and only a faint glow came from slivers of sunlight sneaking through the gaps between the weathered boards of the outside wall. This must have been an old storeroom of some kind.

With cautious, measured steps, he moved forward in the confined space until he reached a small table. His hands stretched out, fingertips brushing over the coarse, splintered edges of the wood. The top was barren except for a thick coat of dust that clung to his skin, offering no tools or hints to help his escape.

Turning his attention to the walls, he ran his fingers along their surface, the rough texture of the unadorned wooden boards beneath his touch. Each of his footsteps echoed, amplifying the terrifying silence when he stopped.

His heart pounded in his chest. The humid air was close, and his breath came short and fast as he worked his way around the room. He ended up at the door. Even though he knew it was a futile gesture, he pulled at it anyway.

His mind darted to Paul. Sooner or later, his brother would come searching for him and most likely end up in the same mess as he was in. He needed to get out now, warn Paul so the two could paddle away from this place.

"Think, Dan, think," he said, forcing himself to take slow, measured breaths as he paced the floor. He thought back to every movie he'd seen, every book he had read, looking for an idea, any idea, for a way out that didn't rely on brute strength or blind luck.

A creak from the old floorboards pulled him from his thoughts. He glanced down, noting the slight bending one gave beneath his weight. Crouching, he inspected closer, running his fingers along the seams where the boards met. They were old, some slightly raised, others worn down from years of being underfoot. It was a long shot, but he recalled the bulkhead doors he had seen outside. There must be a basement under the building — a ready-made escape tunnel.

Energized by that thought, Dan crawled across the floor, his fingers exploring the edges of each plank. His nails snagged on a board with slightly raised ends. A sharp pain shot through his finger as splinters wedged beneath a nail. He quickly withdrew his hand, wincing. This board might be the key. He touched it again, noticing how one end was higher than the adjacent one. If only he could lift it up...

He needed time and luck, but his situation gave him no choice. That board was his only way out. He started to pry it loose.

Chapter Four

Dan's fingers clawed at the narrow gaps surrounding the planks, his nails scratching against the wood. His frustration grew. With a deep sigh, he leaned back on his heels. He couldn't get a firm grip. He needed a tool, something he could use like a crowbar to pry the stubborn floorboard loose.

"There's gotta be something in here that can help me," he said under his breath.

He scanned the room, searching for something useful. The dim light that filtered through the cracks in the board walls gave just enough light to outline the room, but it didn't show any details.

Getting back on his hands and knees, he crawled over the floor once more, examining it inch by inch. Other than his dropped pencil and notebook, he found nothing he could use. Time to try the walls again.

He stood up and went back to them. His fingers glided over the rough wooden boards as he examined each one from top to bottom by touch. After checking the first three walls without finding anything, his fingertips at last brushed something on the last one — a bracket.

An old, rusted L-shaped metal bar stuck out from the wall only a few inches below the ceiling. It might have been used as a shelf support at one time. It had been bolted high enough that Dan figured he must have passed under it during his hurried first search of the room.

Dan's face broke into a smile, a mix of surprise and hope. "Let's give this a try," he said to himself.

His hand clasped the angle bracket, and he gave it a tentative tug. Though it was stubborn and resisted, Dan felt a faint wiggle, perhaps a promise of more movement.

"Come on, you pigheaded hunk of junk," he said, his voice low and strained as he wiggled the bracket side to side.

He paused for a moment, glancing around the room, listening to make sure Rocky hadn't heard any noise. The stillness reassured him, so he went back to work. His muscles ached, but bit by bit, the metal shelf support began to pull loose from its rusty mooring, the wood creaking in reluctant surrender.

With one last twist and yank, the angle bracket came free in Dan's hands. He paused, waiting for Rocky or Mousey to charge into the room through the door. They didn't.

He weighed the piece of metal in his hand. It could be a tool... and if need be, he could stab with it as a weapon. Dan returned the floorboard he had been working on.

Getting on his knees, he wedged one end of the angle bracket into the gap between the floorboards. He pressed down firmly so that the other side of the L-shaped metal rested over the board, like a lever. He grabbed hold and started to jimmy the board up.

The plank creaked softly as it lifted. Dan grinned to himself. It worked! This was it — his chance to escape and go back to Paul.

He shifted his do-it-yourself crowbar to where he guessed the other nail was. He pulled back onto the bracket again. The floorboard released a loud, protesting groan, and the corner popped up. Dan gasped and held his breath, his glance darting again to the door. No sound came from beyond the door.

He jimmied the plank up more. Using his piece of metal as a pry bar, he worked his way around the edges until he pulled the board up from the floor. He put it to one side, revealing an open section big enough for him to slip between the jousts.

Peering down into the darkness below, he steeled his nerves, wondering what waited for him down there. Was it dry? Piles of junk to crash into?

"Maybe there's an alligator waiting for me," Dan thought to himself.

He swung his legs through the opening and was going to drop when he remembered his sketchbook. Shouldn't leave that, he figured. His name and address were written on the first page.

He climbed back out and grabbed the book. How could he keep hold of it when he had to have his hands free to lower himself through the gap? Since he needed both the book and the bracket, he had only one thing to do. He bit the sketchbook with his teeth.

He hooked the angle bracket onto the waistband of his swimsuit. The metal seemed heavy enough to pull his trunks down around his ankles. That would be embarrassing, but he couldn't worry about it now.

Dan squeezed through the narrow opening, lowering his body, his fingers gripping the edge. He let go, landing like a cat on the ground below. As he crouched to absorb the impact, a wave of satisfaction washed over him. The Count of Monte Cristo couldn't have done better.

He stood. However, the angle bracket remained down, dragging Dan's swimsuit to his ankles. His cheeks grew red. He knew it was stupid given his situation, but he couldn't help himself. Putting down his sketchbook, he took the piece of metal out of his waistband, then pulled up his trunks.

His eyes squinted and blinked as they adjusted to the faint light seeping through narrow, dirt-smeared windows. He was in the mill's basement. One wall featured a row of small windows, letting in only weak light because they were filthy or boarded over. Darkness cloaked the basement's far edges, hidden in shadows.

The room was hot, humid and musty. Dan began to sweat.

As he picked up his sketchbook, he noticed a sizable wooden table behind him. Luckily, he had narrowly missed it in his drop from the room upstairs.

Piled high on the top were stacks of paper. A camping lantern dangled above, but Dan had no matches and wasn't about to spend time hunting for any. He bent forward, peering closely at the items on the table in the faint light.

Currency loaded the tabletop. The bills sat in neat, organized piles by denomination, with tens, twenties, fifties, and hundreds, resembling stock on the shelves at the drugstore. He reached out and picked up a bundle, the paper sliding under his fingers. It felt off.

"Fakes," he said in a soft voice, as a shiver crawled up his spine. "These are all counterfeit."

That would explain the printing press upstairs. He had stumbled onto a funny money factory — the very one Ricardo had been searching for. And what better place to hide a counterfeit racket, a more out-of-the-way location, than in the middle of a swamp?

Taking in the size of the bogus fortune on display in front of him, the sheer scale of the operation hit Dan. This wasn't some penny-ante game, no two-bit setup. This was a major undertaking on a national level, just like Ricardo said. No wonder the Treasury Department was flooding the area with agents.

At one end of the table sat some cardboard boxes, about the size of a book, and a roll of packing tape. The fakes must be created here, then shipped off to passers in the rest of the country... maybe even the world.

He had to scram out of here, find Paul and tell Ricardo, he thought. But first, he decided to take some souvenirs.

He carefully slid some fake bills off their stacks and slipped them into his sketchbook. A pencil lay on the table. There could be enough light, he thought. He picked up the pencil and opened his book to a blank page. Squinting in the dim light, he made rough sketches from memory of the faces of Rocky and Mousey. They could help Ricardo.

Dan's mouth went dry. Knowing this information put a target on his back — if Rocky discovered he knew, his life wouldn't be worth the powder to blow it up. He needed to run, get back to Paul, and get out of here.

Putting down the pencil, Dan scouted around, searching for any way out. The nearest small, grimy window was set high on the wall, too narrow for him to pass through. That let the other ones out as well.

There was a wooden staircase, leading to a closed door at the top. He'd bet it was one of the three he'd seen upstairs. The steps dared to creak just because he looked at them.

The only other option was another rickety flight of stairs. They must go to the exterior cellar door, its hinges just visible in the gloom. He weighed his choices.

The hallway door posed the biggest risk — he could stroll right into the counterfeiters' lap. He held the angle bracket like it were a knife. It offered some protection against the intimidating Rocky.

Some, but the bracket may only bend on Rocky's massive frame, much like knives bent off Superman. If that happened, Dan didn't want to think about what Rocky might do to him in return.

That left the cellar door. It was his only chance for a clean getaway. If the bulkhead door wasn't bolted from the outside, that is. He hadn't paid attention when he walked past them outside. There was no need to then, but they were the only viable exit now.

With his mind made up and sketchbook in hand, Dan crept toward the stairs leading to the bulkhead doors. He placed his foot on the first step, and it responded with a loud, groaning shriek that sliced through the stillness. He winced as he prayed to himself that the noise wouldn't attract attention.

It didn't. Perhaps Rocky and Mousey were used to the creaking and groaning of the old building.

As though picking through a minefield, Dan pressed down on each stair, searching for any hint of instability. He climbed one, then the next one, then the next one, until he at last reached the top.

"Be unlocked, be unlocked, be unlocked," he chanted under his breath. Dan grasped the handle and pushed. He grinned as the door swung open.

Poking his head out like a groundhog from its burrow, he squinted in the bright sunlight as he took a moment to get his bearings. The entrance to the mill, about six feet away, was shut. The heavy wooden shutter over the window he had peeked in was also now secured.

Dan emerged from the basement, closing the door with care, cringing at the faint creak it made. Now, to get back to Paul, so they could leave this place and tell the authorities.

That was his plan. But first, he had to reach the canoe without being spotted.

Walking as noiselessly as he could, he headed toward the far end of the mill. He stopped. His gaze moved between the narrow dirt road he used and the thick tangle of trees that encircled the aging structure. The road offered the fastest and most direct escape back to the swamp, but also the most obvious. He hesitated.

Dan wasn't certain how quickly Rocky would discover he had gotten away. He didn't think Rocky was bright enough to light a ten-watt bulb, but wearing a bathing suit could tip Rocky off that

Dan had come from the river area. Rocky would think Dan had taken the road, which was the more straightforward path.

At least, Dan hoped that would be Rocky's assumption. He figured it was safer to sneak back to Paul under the cover of the forest. With that in mind, Dan made his way toward the trees.

He plunged into the tangled undergrowth. He tried to move as quietly as possible, but the forest seemed to have decided something different. Each step triggered rustling branches, snapping twigs, and crunching leaves.

Sunlight filtered through the canopy, casting eerie shadows that made him think he saw the gigantic man lurking behind every tree, every bush, ready to pounce on him like a grizzly bear and pound him into the ground.

In the web of limbs above, birds flitted from limb to limb, their songs of trills and chirps filling the air. Unseen insects orchestrated a constant buzz and rhythmic clicks in the dense underbrush.

Dan scowled. The cheerful sounds of nature were the last thing he wanted to hear while he was fleeing from a dangerous counterfeiting gang.

His grip tightened around the angle bracket in his hand, its cool, solid weight reassuring. He used it and his sketchbook to push aside the low-hanging branches and thorny bushes that blocked his path, moving to get back to Paul and the canoe — fast.

***

Paul let out a yawn, his mouth stretching wide as his fingers scratched at an itch on his stomach. Pulling himself into a seated position, he drew his legs up, hugging them close. He must have dozed off, but he didn't think it was for long.

It was still early, and plenty of light remained until sunset. Still, the brothers still had a good distance to cover before reaching the spot they had planned to make camp for the night. Paul didn't want to fumble with tent poles and stakes in the dark.

"Where is my stupid brother?" Paul grumbled under his breath, getting up from the ground to stretch his legs.

He knew Dan usually lost track of time when he got wrapped up in his art stuff. Paul cupped his hands around his mouth, ready to yell, when a spark of mischief popped into his mind.

Lowering his hands, a sly smile curled up the corners of Paul's lips. "Wait a second. Oh, wait, this is too good to pass up."

Memories of childhood pranks flooded back, vivid and mischievous. Dan had always been a sucker for a good scare. Paul would pop out of closets or sneak up behind his brother with a loud "boo!" to satisfying results. A grin stretched across his face.

"Maybe it's time for Crazy Chester to appear." He chuckled as he envisioned his best insane, murderous old man impression, complete with raspy whispers and a hunched posture. This would be his masterpiece.

He started to follow Dan's trail, his footsteps light and deliberate, able to suppress the excited giggles bubbling up at the thought of his planned trick with great difficulty.

Staying next to the trees and following the old road, he arrived at the mill. He paused for a moment, astonished by the sheer size of the structure in such a remote, marshy wilderness. The building rose before him, its weathered wooden walls towering high against the backdrop of twisted cypress and thick underbrush.

He scanned the area, but he couldn't see Dan. His twin was probably planted on the dirt, cross-legged, on the other side of the building, pencil in hand, his eyes focused on his pad while sketching. Lost in his world of lines and shades, his brother would be oblivious to everything else.

Perfect! It was the perfect setup! A surprise scare was just begging to happen.

Paul jogged to the far end of the mill. Slowing his pace, he craned his neck to peer around the corner. Dan wasn't there. Dan must be at the opposite end from where Paul was now, obscured from view by the building's length, Paul decided. He strode along the wall.

He had almost made it to the end when the mill's door exploded open behind him with a deafening crash. Two figures strode out of the shadows. The first was a towering giant of a man, his broad shoulders nearly blocking the doorway. The other one was younger, smaller, with a crop of curly hair.

"Aren't you glad I checked on him, aren't you, Rocky?" the small kid said in a high-pitched voice.

"Yeah." Rocky's voice, a deep, guttural sound, sent a chill racing down Paul's spine, freezing him in place. "Hey, don't think you're gettin' away from me, Tarzan!"

For a moment, Paul questioned if Dan had spotted him coming and was now trying to pull a prank on him. But that thought quickly fell apart. The kid standing beside the enormous man was definitely not Dan.

Paul had no idea who they were or what they wanted. And he was certain he had no intention of sticking around to find out, however.

He turned, his legs instinctively propelling him back towards the safety of the woods before his mind even seemed to make the choice. His idea was to lose the big gorilla among the trees.

Heavy footsteps pounded behind Paul. Rocky's voice growled, "Come back here, you little punk!"

Paul's heart beat like a drum in his chest as he ran toward the dense forest. He zigzagged, hoping to shake off the pursuers hot on his trail. Risking a quick glance over his shoulder, he caught sight of the huge figure gaining on him despite his size.

Distracted, Paul's foot snagged on a deep rut, and he tumbled forward, hitting the earth hard. The taste of dirt filled his mouth as he tried to rise.

A heavyweight smashed down on his back, driving the air from his lungs and pinning him to the ground. Struggling for release, Paul jabbed his elbow with all his might, feeling the satisfying impact into something solid.

"Oof!" Rocky grunted. "You're gonna pay for that, pal."

Rocky yanked Paul to his feet. His arms were locked behind him in an iron grip that sent a sharp, searing pain through his shoulders as though they were being ripped from their sockets.

Paul jerked his head backward with the power of a sledgehammer. The sickening crack of his skull against the man's chin resonated in the air, causing Rocky's grasp to slacken just enough.

Seizing the moment, Paul wrenched free with a fierce tug. His fist, fueled by adrenaline and anger, fired a right cross at his opponent while he shouted, "Get your dirty paws off of me!" The satisfying thud of his knuckles meeting Rocky's jaw a second time sent a shock wave up his arm, a brief taste of victory.

Rocky's eyes narrowed into fiery slits, his face flushed with anger. Paul barely had time to register the clenched knuckles of Rocky's meaty fist before it swung toward him in a strong uppercut. The next moment, a sharp pain exploded across his jaw, and he tumbled into a void of darkness.

Chapter Five

At last, Dan emerged from the forest and reached the spot where they docked the canoe. Sunlight streamed through the trees, creating a pattern of shadows on the bank next to the swamp.

"Paul," Dan started talking in a harsh whisper before completely clearing the woods, "we gotta beat it! At the mill —"

He stopped and looked around. There was no trace of his brother.

"Paul?" Dan called in a low voice.

Only the rustling leaves and distant bird calls replied. He scanned the area, as if he had somehow made a mistake and didn't spot his six-foot-tall brother the first time. But he hadn't. Paul was gone.

"Now, where did he go? He wouldn't have just wandered off." Dan's fingers raked through his hair in confusion. Then the realization hit him, sharp and sudden, like a punch to the gut. "He must have gone looking for me."

Dan glanced at the old road that led back to the old building. Paul was unaware of the danger waiting at the mill, and now he could be heading smack into it.

Without hesitation, Dan broke into a steady jog. He circled past the canoe, tossing his sketchbook and pencil into it, then headed back down the dirt road he had taken earlier. He didn't know when Paul had left, or even how long it took Dan to escape from the room and get back here. In either case, it meant he had no time to lose.

Each step crunched on fallen leaves, and the sharp crack of snapping twigs sent a jolt of unease up Dan's spine. As he approached the final turn before reaching the mill, he slowed to a walk. He crouched and edged around the curve, eyes checking for any signs of movement. The old structure came into view.

Dan inched up to the weathered building, so tense that any unexpected sight or sound would have launched him to the moon. He swallowed hard, his throat dry as he crept closer to the mill. The rough texture of the wooden boards pressed against his hand as he leaned around the corner, straining to catch any noise from inside the building.

Faint voices drifted out — a deep, gravelly rumble unmistakably belonging to Rocky and a high-pitched, almost squeaky tone that could only be Mousey. Dan listened intently but couldn't hear anybody who sounded like Paul.

Perhaps the brothers had just missed each other, Dan thought, and Paul was already making his way back to the canoe. But Paul also might be a prisoner in the mill, as Dan had been earlier. Which was it?

The only way to figure out the truth meant Dan had to check inside. The door and shutters were shut, so a peek through them was out. That left a single option: to use the way he escaped to go back in. He ran to the basement door.

He pressed his back against the wall, waiting. The sounds of movement still came from the interior, but it seemed nobody had heard his approach. Taking a deep breath, Dan slowly pulled the bulkhead door open, freezing as the rusty hinges let out a sharp, metallic creak.

He slipped through the narrow opening, trying not to move the door any more than necessary. Closing it softly, he blinked as his eyes adjusted to the dim, musty interior. He went down the wooden steps with caution, each one whispering a groan under his weight. At the bottom, he waited again for any sign he'd been spotted. His break-in was successful.

Dan looked up. The floorboard he removed from the room above still wasn't replaced. Then he put together what may have happened. Rocky discovered Dan had escaped and, in the process, knew he had come across the fake money. Rocky went searching for Dan but, unfortunately, encountered Paul instead. Since Paul didn't have his glasses on, and both the identical twins wore navy blue swim trunks and sneakers, Rocky must have mistaken Paul for Dan.

But where was his brother now? In the same room Rocky had locked Dan in earlier, maybe tied up? He concentrated, but there wasn't any movement from where he had been kept prisoner. He shook his head. That didn't make any sense anyway. Rocky wouldn't put Paul in a room that already had a ready-made escape hatch. So, his brother must be somewhere else in the building.

Dan looked around the basement until he saw a door he didn't notice the first time he was down there. Was Paul in there? He slipped across the floor and turned the doorknob. He winced as the door opened with a groan.

He froze again. Everything in this place creaked, rattled or squeaked. Still no sound came from upstairs, so he hoped the noise hadn't been picked up.

Beyond the doorway lay a windowless room, the air heavy and dense. He entered, nearly hitting his head on a rusted pipe hanging from the ceiling. Directly in front of him, he could just make out the bulky shape of an old boiler. Dan spoke into the darkness, "Paul? Are you in here, buddy? Let me know if you are. Move if you can."

No answer. Dan squinted, but couldn't see anything that looked like a person. He needed to check the floor above.

Closing the door, he moved to the other staircase, his footsteps light as he climbed, pressing himself close to the edge to minimize any groaning wooden steps. When he reached the top, he gently eased the door open to a tiny slit.

His earlier suspicions proved correct. He was at the middle door, which opened into the hallway. The room where he had been held captive was just a few feet away on his left. Wedging himself between the frame and the door, he scrunched, so he could peer into the office. The sight that met his eyes confirmed his worst fears.

Paul hung from the ceiling. Ropes bound his wrists tightly together, and he was suspended from a rusty hook embedded high above. His arms strained upward, and his toes barely touched the floor. A cloth gag was secured around his mouth. Meanwhile, Rocky sat close by, reading a crime pulp magazine. After a few minutes, he tossed it aside in disgust.

"Aw, them writers know nothin' about nothin'," he complained. He watched something going on that Dan couldn't see. "You're gonna polish that machine so much, there'll be nothin' left, Mousey."

The young boy came into view, rag in one hand. He beamed at Rocky's compliment. "Yeah! But she sure looks sharp, doesn't she?"

Rocky leaned forward and grinned. "You break it, and the Professor will have our hides."

"Don't worry, Rocky. Machines and I get along great!" Mousey stepped out of sight again, probably to resume his polishing.

Dan's fists clenched at his sides. How could he free Paul with those two in the same room? He needed a plan, and fast. The crunch of gravel outside made him stop. Muffled voices approached the mill. Heart pounding, Dan closed the door to the barest of openings.

The front door swung open with a bang. "We're back!" a gruff voice called out.

"About time," Rocky said from the office. "Did you bring everything, Vic?"

Two men Dan didn't recognize entered, carrying boxes. The taller one dumped his load on the floor with a thud. He removed his worn-out fedora and wiped his forehead with a handkerchief. The man was of average height with a wiry build, with sharp features and piercing eyes that seemed to assess every situation for potential profit or danger. Despite wearing a cheap pinstripe suit, the heat and humidity didn't appear to bother him much. Dan got the impression that nothing much did.

"Yeah, yeah, keep your pants on," Vic said. "This paper is heavy."

The second man was around six feet tall. A size-too-small shirt, with the top three buttons open, accented his muscular physique. The long sleeves were folded halfway up his forearms, and shiny tonic slicked down his black hair. He wore a constant smirk that broadcast a cocky attitude, his eyes dark and shrewd. He was only a year or two older than Dan. "Where's the kid?" he asked.

"Here I am, Tommy." Mousey appeared in the doorway.

Tommy tossed a smaller box to Mousey. "Here's that roller you wanted."

Mousey caught the container. "Great! This'll make the press run real smooth." He bustled back to the machine.

With a grunt, Vic and Tommy picked up the other boxes, taking them into the office. After putting them against the wall, Tommy noticed Paul.

"Who's this mug?" Tommy swaggered over to him.

"Found him sneaking around the joint," Rocky answered. "He's slippery, so he's in here, where I can keep an eye on 'em."

"How about it, pal?" Tommy gave Paul's head a shove. "What's the idea, sticking your nose in where it's not supposed to be, huh?"

Paul glared at Tommy.

Tommy turned to speak to the others and laughed. "Hey... hey! Maybe he's a cop... or a G-man?" He pushed Paul's head again. "How about it, punk? Are you a cop or G-man?"

"So what do we do with him?" Vic spoke to Rocky, jerking his head toward Paul.

"Let the Professor decide," Rocky said.

"Want me to find out why he's here?" Tommy pulled out a switchblade, flicking it open. He made a few slashing motions in the air with the knife. "I'll make him talk... fast."

"Oh, put the blade away," Vic said in a weary voice. He tugged at his collar. "Damn, it's hot in here. Can't we open a window?"

Rocky tilted his head toward Paul. "That's how he got an eyeful. The windows stay shut. The Professor wants it that way."

"Who says you're in charge when the Professor is away?" Vic challenged.

Rocky stood up, towering over Vic. He jerked his thumb at himself and spoke with the threatening menace of somebody used to being obeyed and not questioned. "Me, that's who."

"Okay, okay." Vic waved Rocky off. "I'm going upstairs to grab some shuteye."

Pulling the door closed, Dan held his breath as Vic passed his hiding spot. Another door opened — the one to his right — and Vic's footsteps mounted some stairs, going to the second floor.

Dan had to do something, but what? He looked down at the angle bracket he still gripped in his hand. It was a weapon, sort of. But even with that, the odds ran four against one.

Unless...

A wild idea took shape in Dan's mind. It was risky, but it might be their only chance. He crept back to the bulkhead door, easing it wide enough to slip outside. He ran to the open end of the building and up to the huge saw blade. Banging on it with the angle bracket, he then raced to the edge of the forest. Almost immediately, confused voices came from inside the mill.

Taking a deep breath, Dan cupped his hands around his mouth and let go of an insane laugh, as though he were Crazy Chester.

"What the hell?" Rocky shouted from inside.

Dan didn't wait. Again, he cut loose with a second yell, praying it sounded like it came from a different direction. He heard the mill door bang open.

"Someone's out there!" Vic shouted.

"It came from down there!" yelled Tommy.

"Spread out!" Rocky ordered. "Find whoever it was!"

Dan fired off the angle bracket from waist high with all his might. It crashed through some brush before splashing into the swamp water.

"Over there!" Tommy cried. "He's running through the brush!"

Dan ducked behind a shrub. He allowed himself a whisper of a breath as the gang members emerged from behind the decrepit mill, their footsteps pounding on the ground like distant thunder. Rocky continued yelling instructions, tearing through the dense tangle of bushes and snapping twigs as they hunted for the elusive, non-existent trespasser.

As soon as they entered the forest and disappeared from view, Dan dashed toward the door. His hands trembled slightly as he pushed it open, slipping quietly back into the silent, now deserted building.

"Paul!" Dan hissed, rushing to his twin's side. He grabbed his brother around his waist. "When I lift, try to unhook yourself. Go!"

With a grunt, Dan hoisted Paul up, loosening the tension on the hook. Paul unhooked the rope, and Dan let him down to the floor. He fumbled with the tight knots binding Paul's wrists. "Hang on. I've got you," Dan whispered, freeing Paul's hands. He yanked the gag from his brother's mouth. "Are you okay?"

Paul nodded. "What's this all about?"

"This place is counterfeiter HQ," Dan said. "Let's make tracks..."

They burst through the door into the hot, humid air. A shout shattered the silence.

"Hey, look! There are two of 'em!"

Dan's blood ran cold as he turned to see Rocky and Mousey at the corner of the mill, pointing at the brothers. Vic and Tommy came right behind them.

Rocky's face contorted with rage. "Grab 'em!" He charged toward the brothers like a bull.

"Come on." Dan gripped his brother's elbow to steady him. "Let's scram out of here."

"No need to tell me that twice," Paul said. The twins took off to the trees, their sneakers slapping against the hard-packed earth.

"They're still in back of us," Paul panted, not wasting energy to look back.

Dan risked a glance over his shoulder. Rocky and Mousey were closing in on the brothers — Rocky's barrel chest heaved with effort, while Mousey's thin frame proved deceptively quick as he gained ground.

The patch of dry land was small, perhaps a few hundred yards across at its widest point, surrounded by the murky embrace of the swamp. The mill squatted at its center like a forgotten monument, and their way out — the canoe — waited at the ruins of the dock. If they could reach it before the gang caught them...

"We're going to make it," Dan said, forcing confidence into his voice. The words came out staccato between labored breaths.

They reached the edge of the clearing, where the dirt gave way to scattered trees. The brothers plunged into the woods. Although the relative shade offered no relief from the heat and humidity, it did provide momentary cover from the gang as they dodged and weaved around the trunks. Dan oriented himself — the river should be straight ahead, through increasingly dense vegetation.

Then he saw them — two figures cutting through the woods on their left. Vic's silhouette was unmistakable, even at that distance. Beside him moved Tommy, no less threatening.

"Stop." Dan threw out an arm to halt Paul's momentum.

They ducked behind the wide trunk of a water oak, breathing hard, their bodies pressed against the rough bark. For a moment, the trees shielded them from their pursuers, who remained twenty yards behind them.

"A couple of them must have circled around," Dan said in a quiet voice. "They're trying to cut us off... flush us out."

Dan dared to peer around the tree's edge. Rocky and Mousey advanced with hunters' precision, their eyes sweeping the trees where the twins had vanished into the shadows. On the opposite flank, Vic and Tommy fanned out, forming a deadly pincer movement. The gang closed in from both sides like commandos, tightening the noose and trying to ensnare Dan and Paul.

"They're not going to give up," Dan said. He knew counterfeit money meant federal charges — years in prison if they're caught. The gang had too much to lose to let the brothers get away.

"We need to split them up," Paul said. "Make them chase us in different directions."

Dan nodded his agreement.

"We separate. You go left, and I'll go right." Paul cast a glance at the approaching figures.

"Well, we wanted to tour the swamp," Dan said, giving a weak grin.

"Remember to send me a postcard," Paul replied. "Whoever gets to the canoe first goes for help. Don't wait for the other. Okay?"

"But —"

"Okay? Don't wait," Paul stressed.

Dan swallowed. "Okay." He clasped his brother's shoulder, meeting his eyes. "Be careful," he said, the words inadequate for all that he felt.

Paul's face showed a strange mixture of fear and determination that Dan suspected mirrored his own. "You too."

Without another word, the twins separated — Paul veering left, and Dan curving right.

***

Dan slowed as he had to pick through the trees and bushes that became thicker. The humidity pressed down on him. Sweat trickled down his spine, and he was suddenly very aware of his exposed state — wearing nothing but his swim trunks and sneakers. For some reason, he remembered a short story he read in high school English class: "The Most Dangerous Game,"... a tale of a man being tracked by a professional hunter. At the time, he thought it was silly and unrealistic. He changed his mind now.

His sneakers slipped on the dirt as he navigated around a group of cypress trees. Ahead, the earth sloped into a hollow of a dark, sticky patch of mud, where the swamp was trying to take over a patch of dry ground. Dan's eyes lingered on this scene as a plan began to take shape. Beyond the mud, a chaotic network of drooping branches formed a natural barricade.

"Perfect," he said to himself.

Dan paused, listening. The shouts had grown more distant but were still there — angry voices calling to each other, the occasional crack of a branch as the gang pushed through the woods. He had a limited amount of time to do something.

Stepping to the edge of the muddy patch, he calculated what to do next. The trick wasn't just to leave tracks but to leave the correct kind of tracks. They had to be obvious enough to be followed, but also messed up enough to suggest panic. He placed his right foot firmly in the gunk. He pressed down harder than necessary, forming a deep, unmistakable footprint.

"This has to work," he muttered, methodically placing one foot after another, making a distinct trail leading directly toward the thicket of branches.

Dan reached the edge of the cluster of branches and deliberately snapped the first limb. He pressed on, snapping one branch after another, leaving clear signs of someone pushing through. The coarse wood scraped against his bare chest, leaving thin red marks, but he paid no mind to the sting. Every broken branch was a signal: someone rushed through here.

Dan worked like the artist he was, creating just the right amount of disturbance, while being careful not to actually create a path that would make pursuit too easy. When he'd gone a few feet in, he backed out carefully, stepping only in his existing footprints.

He stopped, crouching behind a massive bush, and listened. The voices were close — he recognized Rocky's gruff commands and Mousey's squeaky replies. They were coming nearer, but they still hadn't spotted him yet.

"... can't have gotten far." Rocky's voice carried through the dense forest.

"I thought I heard something," Mousey said. "Over there."

Soon, Rocky and Mousey would stumble across the mud patch and the broken branches. He had laid his diversion. Now all that he had to do was to see if it worked.

Mousey appeared first, his small frame threading the foliage like a thread through a needle. The huge Rocky lumbered behind him, crashing through the brush with the grace of an elephant. The two halted where the natural path through the trees stopped dead.

"What the —" Rocky's words died as he stared at the bewildering maze of intertwined wood in front of him.

"There, Rocky, look!" Mousey crouched and pointed to a partial footprint in the soft earth. "He went this way. See? Here are his tracks." He rose, stepped through the mud and examined the bushes. "And look! Some branches are broken! He must've come this way! See, Rocky? See?"

"We should have taken them out when we had the chance," Rocky grumbled. "Once I catch them, they'll be sorry I didn't just shoot them. Maybe I will anyway."

"You wanted the Professor to decide what to do with them. Remember?" Mousey said, his voice anxious. "I heard you say that. That's what you said. Clear as day. You said, 'Let the Pro—'"

Rocky cuffed Mousey on his temple. "Shut yer face! I recollect what I said," he growled. "Okay, okay, get movin'. He's gettin' away."

Mousey squeezed through the bramble. "It's open on the other side, Rocky."

Rocky forced his massive body through the tangled branches, flinging curses as he went.

Dan didn't breathe until the noise of Rocky and Mousey rustling through the undergrowth faded. Only then did he allow himself to smile. He set off in another direction, wondering how Paul was getting on... or if he would ever see him again.

Chapter Six

The forest floor passed under Paul's feet in a blur of rotting leaves and exposed roots, all threatening to trip him. The crashes and curses of Vic and Tommy pushed through the trees behind him, too close for comfort but growing more distant with every passing second. For some reason, Paul thought about when he and Dan played army when they were kids, the fun they had stalking the other one through their neighborhood... except now it was no game.

The underbrush was a thick weave of bushes, their branches reaching out like hands with grasping fingers, eager to hold him back. His bare torso bore the evidence of his struggle — thin red lines etched across his skin where sharp twigs had clawed at him. Yet, despite the scratches, the sting didn't register to him.

A fallen log appeared in his path, covered with moss and partially rotted. Without breaking stride, Paul gathered himself and leaped, sailing over the obstacle with inches to spare. His landing was nearly silent, the balls of his feet absorbing the impact before he went off again, already scanning the terrain ahead.

The forest was thickest here, away from the mill and its clearing. Years of no logging had allowed nature to reclaim the land with zeal. Young trees grew at odd angles, fighting for patches of sun. The canopy overhead filtered the sunlight into a green-gold patchwork that dappled the ground, making the shadows sway with each breeze.

Behind him, Paul heard a crash and a string of profanity. A smile flashed across his face, there and gone in an instant. Vic or Tommy had found the log the hard way.

"He went this way!" Tommy's voice carried through the woods, strained and angry.

"I can see that," Vic replied calmly. "I'm not blind."

Paul used their bickering voices to gauge distance. Too close. He needed to widen the gap.

His path ahead narrowed, squeezed tightly by a thicket of young pines. The trees intertwined to create a formidable barricade on either side. Paul squinted a little, trying to force his eyes into focus, as he gazed anxiously around, hoping to spot an escape. The dense foliage revealed no gaps. It was as if nature had crafted a narrow funnel, forcing him forward.

He had no other choice. Lowering his head, he pushed into the tight passage, skinny enough that his bare shoulders still brushed the pine needles. The sharp scent of sap filled his nostrils, mingling with the musty odor of decaying vegetation underfoot.

The way through the trees was longer than it appeared, twisting slightly before widening again into a small clearing. Paul burst into the open space and immediately dodged right, circling back along the edge of the thicket. If he moved quickly, Vic and Tommy would continue straight, assuming he'd done the same.

He crouched in back of a bush, his breathing controlled, quiet gasps. Sweat trickled down his back and chest, pooling at the waistband of his swimsuit. Within seconds, the sounds of pursuit grew louder. Vic emerged first from the narrow path, his tall frame stooped from ducking under branches. He paused, eyes scanning the area with the focus of a wolf.

Tommy stumbled out behind him, nearly colliding with Vic's back. His face was flushed an alarming shade of crimson, his breath coming in wheezing gulps. He bent forward, his hands on his knees. "Where'd he go?"

Vic raised a finger to his lips, head tilted slightly as he listened. Paul pressed his body deeper into the shadow of the shrub.

"He kept going." Vic pointed across the clearing to where the ground sloped downward. "Look at the plants there. They're still moving."

Paul risked a glance and grinned. The foliage Vic pointed to did sway gently, disturbed by nothing more than a passing breeze. But Vic's mistake worked in his favor. Perhaps nature was coming over to his side at last.

"You sure?" Tommy straightened up, wiping sweat from his forehead with the back of his hand. "I don't think —"

"You ain't got the brains to think." Vic started striding toward the other end of the clearing. "Come on. He couldn't have gone far."

Tommy followed, muttering something under his breath that Paul couldn't catch. The two crossed the open space and disappeared down the slope into the woods again.

Paul allowed himself three slow breaths before setting into motion again. Vic's error had bought him some time, but they'd realize their mistake soon enough.

He set off at a right angle, moving parallel to the slope, plunging back into the thick undergrowth. Leaves brushed against his calves, leaving smears of moisture on his already dirty skin. The ground beneath his feet grew increasingly spongy, a warning that the land he was on may not be as dry as he thought. Meaning he was headed back toward the swamp.

A surge of hope pushed Paul forward. The brothers agreed to meet back at the canoe when separated. That was the plan. Return to the canoe and paddle to get help. Both of them, he hoped. He shook his head. No, despite what he had said earlier, the two were leaving together. He refused to leave Dan.

***

The ground grew soft under Dan's sneakers, sucking at his feet with his steps, perhaps a sign that he was approaching the swamp. He ducked and wove, moving in the opposite direction of the shouts, hoping the dense vegetation would hide him. Every crack of a twig he stepped on sounded impossibly loud, almost like sending up a flare of his location, and he winced at each noise.

The voices of his pursuers became louder, closer, like baying hounds. He heard Rocky berating Mousey; his voice was sharp and accusatory, slicing through the hot air like an arrow. "You let him get away, you idiot!"

Dan's heart sank; they were catching up. He pushed on, desperate to put more distance between them, but he was clear he was losing ground. The heat and humidity weighed him down, smothering him, but he forced his legs to keep moving.

He stopped and looked back, peering over a bush to see how close they were. Rocky spotted him, a triumphant shout escaping his lips. "There he is!"

Dan felt a stab of panic. He couldn't let them catch him. He turned, running as fast as he could, crashing through the underbrush, not caring now how much noise he created. His breath came in ragged gasps, and every muscle screamed in protest, but he didn't slow down. He couldn't afford to.

He continued on until he encountered a large fallen tree, almost stumbling into a hole that was in front of it. An idea popped into his mind immediately.

A few branches, still with some dried leaves clinging to them, were scattered by the log, broken off when the tree crashed down. In a rush, he hauled and dragged these to the trunk, using them to conceal the opening. Then, he sprinted around the tree and crouched behind a bush. Rocky and Mousey were approaching fast. Dan had set the trap, and he was the bait.

Rocky and Mousey reached the log, their breath coming in heavy gasps, their frustration obvious. The fallen tree loomed before them, an unexpected barrier in their path. From his hiding place, Dan could see the confusion flicker across their faces as they wondered which way he had gone. Time to give them a hint... and snap the trap. Dan popped up from behind the bush.

Rocky pointed at him. "There he is!"

Mousey charged ahead, his eyes fixed on Dan. As he sprinted, his foot came down hard on a tangle of branches concealing the hole in front of a fallen log. He pitched forward. Rocky, who was close on Mousey's heels, didn't have time to react. He tripped over Mousey's sprawled form and went tumbling headfirst over the log, his arms flailing as he tried unsuccessfully to regain his balance. He ended up in a bush, headfirst.

"Why don't you watch where you're goin'!" Rocky snapped as he tried to regain his footing. "Get up, you fool."

"Sorry, Rocky," Mousey mumbled.

Dan couldn't help but laugh as he took off, darting out of sight behind the undergrowth. The canoe was his target. It was his only chance to escape, and, as the saying goes, time was of the essence. He sprinted as fast as he could, moving over the rough terrain, weaving around branches and bushes. The forest became just blots of green and brown as he pushed himself forward.

The edge of the swamp appeared abruptly, as if the solid earth surrendered all at once to the murky water. Dan skidded to a stop and looked around, finally deciding to head to his left. He followed the swamp's ragged shore, his feet squelching in the increasingly soft earth.

Then, through a gap in the cypress trees, he saw it — a glimpse of the birch in the sunlight. The canoe! It rested at its moorings at the old dock.

Twenty yards. That's all that separated him from freedom.

A chorus of frogs fell silent as he approached, their bulging eyes tracking his progress from lily pads and half-submerged logs.

Fifteen yards. He was going to make it.

Ten yards. He decided he would paddle away in the canoe until he was out of sight. When Paul showed up, he would try to return and pick him up.

Five yards. Rocky's voice sounded from behind him: "Hold it, you!"

***

Paul froze in his tracks, his heart pounding in his chest. The voices of Vic and Tommy echoed through the dense forest, growing louder with each passing second. The rustling leaves and snapping twigs under their feet broadcast their approach... directly toward him.

He squinted through the thick underbrush. How did this happen? Did they circle back, did he, or did they both? Whatever it was, the result was the same. He knew that if he didn't change direction immediately, he would collide with them head-on. Should he go to the left? To the right? Then he realized there was one way he hadn't tried: up.

His eyes locked onto the low-hanging branch of a cottonwood tree. Without a second thought, he leapt, his hands closing around the limb. It bent slightly under his weight, but held firm. He pulled himself up swiftly and kept climbing the trunk, his movements sure and fluid, until he disappeared into the dense canopy.

The world below faded as Paul settled into his perch. He peered down through the screen of leaves, his breath steady, his heart a quiet drum. The sounds of pursuit grew nearer, and soon he could make out the figures of Vic and Tommy, their voices rising above the rustle of the underbrush. They reached the base of the tree.

"He's gotta be around here somewhere." Tommy kicked at the dirt, his temper flaring. "I'm getting tired of this."

Vic shook his head. "You're always in too much of a hurry, kid," he said, his voice taunting. "We'll get him. Just have to be smart about it."

Tommy's frustration seemed to radiate from him like intense heat. He came to a sudden halt, his eyes fiercely sweeping over the underbrush. He crouched down, grabbed a rock, and threw it into the bushes with all his strength. The sound was sharp and abrupt, causing a flock of birds to burst into the sky.

Vic chuckled, rich with amusement. "You're such a hothead," he said, shaking his head at Tommy's outburst. "It's gonna get you in trouble one of these days. Let's go, killer."

Paul stayed still, his body a part of the branch, invisible and patient. Vic and Tommy didn't look up, too caught in their own noise and bluster to notice their target hidden above.

The two went on. Paul remained where he was, suspended in the branches, waiting for the forest to swallow them completely before he dared to move. He began his descent on the opposite side of the tree. His movements were careful and controlled, each step planned to avoid detection. The rough bark guided him back to the ground.

He landed softly, the earth damp and yielding under his feet. Paul stayed down, his eyes tracking Vic and Tommy as they moved further away, still caught up in their argument.

He allowed himself a small, triumphant smile as they disappeared deeper into the forest. Relief washed over him, a brief, calming wave that broke as his eyes spotted something else, something that sent a chill racing down his spine.

Coiled among the gnarled roots, only a foot or so away, a copperhead snake lay motionless, its scales a perfect pattern of browns and creams. The light through the canopy fragmented across its skin, a shifting, hypnotic play of color that seemed almost unreal. For a moment, Paul could do nothing but stare, the world narrowing to the silent, dangerous beauty of the reptile before him.

The snake's forked tongue flicked out, a quicksilver flash that sent a jolt through Paul, a warning as clear as a shout. He froze, every muscle locked in place, his breath caught somewhere between fear and awe.

***

Rocky's voice boomed out. "Stop, I said!"

The canoe was within reach, a slender shape against the water's edge. Dan pushed himself harder, the promise of escape a matter of strides away. He was almost there, almost safe.

Rocky emerged from the cover of the woods, his hulking silhouette menacing in the sunlit clearing. Mousey popped out behind him. Rocky was closer to the canoe than Dan was.

"Hold it right there, Tarzan!" Rocky's order was a force that demanded obedience. He must have figured out Dan's goal, and he also started for the canoe.

Rocky would beat Dan there, but Dan couldn't stop. He wouldn't stop. The water called to him, a last chance shimmering under the relentless sun.

If he couldn't reach the canoe, the swamp was still there, still promising escape. He could swim away. Go underwater. He couldn't be spotted below the murky surface. Dan turned sharply, his feet slapping the ground in a desperate bid for freedom.

"Get him, Mousey!" Rocky's command sliced through the tension like a whip.

Dan reached the water's edge. He splashed in; the cold water surged around his shoes. For a moment, he thought he might make it. Maybe he could reach the canoe after all.

But Mousey was on him in an instant, tackling him at the knees. Dan twisted, thrashed, his limbs a flurry of wild motion as he tried to break free. Mousey grunted and clung on, refusing to let go. Their feet churned the water around their feet, a wild, chaotic struggle and resistance. The two tumbled into the swamp.

Dan fought with everything he had, his breath coming in ragged bursts. But Mousey's determination made up for his lack of physical size and suddenly seemed to have grown more arms than an octopus. The two rolled over and over in the murky water. Inevitably, Dan felt himself being forced under the surface.

The world went into a bubbly silence, the water closing over his head. Mousey held him down. Panic surged through Dan, a primal terror that screamed for air. He kicked, clawed, his movements growing weaker as Mousey kept him underwater, the pressure building in his lungs like a ticking bomb. Dan's mind was a whirl of fear and desperation, a drowning man's final, futile rebellion against the inevitable.

Dan's resistance crumbled, the last of his strength ebbing away like the ripples on the water's surface. His body went limp. Mousey must have felt the change, the fight leaving Dan as suddenly as it had begun. Mousey dragged him onto the shore. Air rushed into Dan's lungs, a painful, desperate gulp.

He blinked, water streaming down his face, blurring the world into a smear of light and shadow. Rocky towered over him. The power was all his now, Dan's brief hope of escape gone.

Mousey stood proudly. "I did good, didn't I? Huh, Rocky? Didn't I? I did good?"

"Yeah, you did good." Rocky glared at Dan. "On your feet, Tarzan."

Dan slowly climbed to his feet.

Rocky looked him up and down. "Why didn't you tell me there were two of you?"

"You never asked," Dan fired back.

Mousey snickered. Rocky backhanded him across the face. Mousey staggered back, one hand rubbing his reddening cheek.

"Leave him alone," Dan barked.

"Who's gonna stop me?" Rocky mocked. "You?"

Dan pulled himself up to his full height. "Yeah. Me."

Rocky took out a snub-nosed revolver from his pocket and pointed it at Dan. "How about now, hero? You gonna stop me now?" He waited a second, then roared with derisive laughter. "Didn't think so. Courage slinks away at the point of a gun." He glanced at the canoe. "Punch a hole in it," he ordered Mousey, his voice as steady and deadly as the weapon in his hand.

Mousey nodded, still rubbing his cheek. "Yeah, Rocky, 'course, Rocky. Right away." Digging out a partially buried stone, he waded to the canoe. He raised the rock, the motion deliberate and final, and brought it down with a savage force. Again, and again, and again.

The wood split with a splintering crack that reverberated across the still water. Mousey untied the rope from the old dock. With a shove, he sent the canoe drifting away from the shore, its hull starting to sag under the weight of water seeping through its fractured side.

As the canoe slowly sank, Mousey straightened up, his face alight with a satisfied grin. He returned to where Rocky waited.

Rocky motioned with his gun. "Okay, punk, you've caused me a lot of trouble. As much as I'd like to take care of you now, I've gotta wait for the Professor." He grabbed Dan's arm with a firm and unyielding grip, pulling and then shoving Dan back toward the mill, away from the water's edge, away from any chance of escape. "Get movin'."

Dan gave a fleeting glance over his shoulder at the sunken canoe. The sight was a reminder of his failure... to himself and Paul. He lowered his head and stumbled along, a captive once more in the ruthless grasp of the counterfeiters.

He hoped his brother could find another way out...

Chapter Seven

Dan stumbled over the uneven forest floor, the damp leaves clinging to his shoes as Rocky jabbed the cold barrel of the gun into his spine.

"Keep movin'," Rocky said, his voice like gravel underfoot. "Almost there."

Mousey scurried ahead, his small frame darting between trees with the agility of his namesake. Dan's brain raced through possible ways to escape, each one more desperate than the last. The revolver at his back chased all those thoughts out of his mind, though. One wrong move and — well, he didn't want to think about that.

Emerging from the dense, shadowy forest, they stepped into the bright sunlight. The old mill's imposing structure loomed before them. The windows, barred with rusted iron shutters, reminded Dan less of a place where cypress logs were once cut and more of a prison. His prison.

Dan wondered if he should try to make a break for it, eyeing the undergrowth to his right. His muscles tensed, ready to spring, but Rocky seemed to sense his intentions.

"Don't even think about it, Tarzan," Rocky said. "You ain't gettin' away by swingin' through the trees on a vine." He chuckled at his own wit. The gun barrel dug deeper into Dan's back, a cold promise that stopped any ideas of running.

"Eyes forward." Rocky shoved Dan toward the mill's entrance. The wooden door creaked on its rusted hinges, providing a mournful welcome as Mousey pushed it open. The sound echoed through the interior, disturbing a flutter of wings somewhere in the rafters above.

They stepped back into the shadows of the mill once more. Mousey hurried over to the door of the room where Dan had been held before, then stopped. "Wait. There's a hole in the floor in there, Rocky."

"I know. Downstairs instead," Rocky said.

"Okay," Mousey said. He opened the middle door.

"Down there," Rocky gestured with his chin toward the narrow staircase that descended into the basement. All three headed through the door, the steps groaning under their weight.

"Where are you going to put him?" Mousey asked.

"The boiler room," Rocky answered. "The door's the only way in and out. There's no window in there. Get the lantern. "

Mousey scrambled for the camp lantern hanging from a hook screwed over the table. Lighting it, he went to the room door and flung it open.

"Inside." Rocky nudged Dan forward with the gun.

The massive cast-iron boiler dominated the center, glinting in the light of the lantern. Its gauge faces were shattered, the needles frozen at readings taken decades ago. A maze of pipes sprawled outward from the boiler, some as thick as Dan's torso, others slender as his wrist, all wrapped in the tattered remnants of insulation that hung like peeling skin. Water dripped somewhere in the darkness.

Dan eyed the room's confined space, his stomach tightening as Rocky shoved him farther into the room. The lantern cast grotesque shadows that twisted across the walls, transforming the rusted pipes into writhing serpents. The air was heavy with the scent of abandonment, tinged with something metallic that made Dan's throat constrict. He turned around to face his captor.

"Are you going to lock him in here, Rocky?" Mousey asked.

"Nah. The door won't lock." Rocky's eyes narrowed, studying Dan with cold calculation. "Mousey," he barked. "Grab that roll of packing tape from the table out there."

"Sure thing, Rocky." Mousey nodded vigorously.

"And hurry. Our friend may be getting ideas again. I can see it in his eyes." Rocky sneered, keeping the gun trained at Dan's heart.

Mousey scurried away, his footsteps tracing his progress through the basement beyond, followed by the sound of rummaging through the counterfeiting supplies, papers shuffling, a chair scraping against concrete, and a few muttered curses as he searched. "Found it!"

"About time," Rocky complained.

Mousey reappeared in the doorway, clutching a thick roll of industrial duct tape that gleamed dully in the lantern light.

"Take care of him." Rocky's lips curled into a smile that never reached his eyes. "And Mousey, make sure this time our guest doesn't get loose. You understand me?"

Mousey's thin face was pulled tight with anxiety. "I got it, Rocky. I'll do it right."

"You better," Rocky growled. "Because if he gets away again, you won't."

Mousey swallowed hard, audible in the tense silence. His hands trembled a little as he tore off a strip of tape with his teeth, a loud ripping sound that sliced through the stagnant air. He walked up to Dan.

"On the floor. Lie down. Face first," Mousey ordered Dan, his voice attempting authority but wavering at the edges. His eyes pleaded with Dan to obey.

Dan hesitated, measuring the distance to the door, calculating his odds. The gun in Rocky's hand shifted, the barrel now aimed at his kneecap. And the big man blocked the doorway. There was no way out.

Dan got down on his knees and then lowered himself to the ground, his palms pressed against the cold, gritty concrete. A fine layer of soot and decades of dirt coated his skin. Tiny pieces of gravel bit into his flesh as he lay face down, shivering at the coldness of the cement.

"Hands together," Mousey's voice cracked slightly. "Behind your back."

Dan did so, bringing his wrists next to each other in the small of his back. The muscles in his shoulders protested, a dull ache spreading across his upper back as his bare chest pressed harder against the unforgiving floor.

Mousey knelt beside him. "Don't move," he said so softly that Dan wasn't sure if he was being instructed or if Mousey was reassuring himself.

The first contact of the tape touching Dan's skin was cold and alien. Mousey started at his wrists and wrapped them methodically, the adhesive making a sick, slithering sound as it unraveled from the roll. Around and around it went, each layer binding Dan's hands more completely than the last. Mousey worked with precision, his trembling fingers becoming steadier with every rotation, as though repeating the task calmed his nerves.

"Tighter," Rocky said from his position by the door.

Mousey responded by yanking the next loop so tightly that Dan let out a gasp as the tape dug into his skin. The binding progressed beyond his wrists, moving toward his fingers, encasing his hands together like a mummy. The tape spiraled from his wrists to his fingertips, turning Dan's hands into an ineffective silver club. Each finger was pressed tightly against the next, immobilized in a sheath of industrial-strength adhesive.

Even in the dim light, Dan saw the sweat beading on Mousey's upper lip, catching the glow of the lantern like tiny jewels. Mousey's eyes darted occasionally to Rocky, seeking approval, then back to his job.

"Good," Rocky nodded, satisfaction evident in his voice. "Now, the legs."

"Ankles together," Mousey spoke with a steadier tone now, as though emboldened by Rocky's approval.

Dan hesitated, his leg muscles tensing. This was it — his last chance to resist before complete immobilization. The only sounds in the room were the distant drip of water and Rocky's measured breathing.

"I said, ankles together!" Mousey said with a new edge to his tone. He glanced nervously at Rocky, who shifted his weight, bored.

Dan slid his feet together, and Mousey began to work on Dan's ankles, the tape making that same wet hiss as it came off the spool. Each wrapped circuit was methodical and precise. Mousey worked with the concentration of an artist, his tongue caught between his teeth as he labored.

"Make sure it's good and tight," Rocky directed, his gravelly voice steady and firm from where he stood in the doorway. The glow of the lantern flickered, casting his rugged features into stark canyons of light and dark. His eyes, half-illuminated, scrutinized Mousey's work, making sure no detail was overlooked.

"It's okay. I got it, Rocky." Mousey yanked the adhesive with renewed vigor. The pressure around Dan's ankles increased.

"That's enough on the legs," Rocky said after what seemed like hours. "Gag him."

Mousey rolled Dan onto his back, then tore off two more pieces of tape. He pressed them across Dan's mouth, taking care to press down all the edges for a good seal. Finishing, he got up and hurried back to Rocky. He spoke with some pride as he gestured toward

Dan. "I did good, huh, Rocky? Didn't I? When I tie somebody up, they stay tied up."

"Yeah, you did good," Rocky said.

"What's... what's gonna happen to him now?" Mousey asked. His fingers fiddled with the roll of tape, turning it in circles.

Rocky shrugged.

"Are you... I mean... will he be... be hurt?" Mousey glanced at Dan with some sympathy showing in his eyes.

"How should I know? Stop askin' me stupid questions! What happens to him will be up to the Professor!" Rocky eyed Dan. "But it won't be pretty, I can say that."

"Yeah, right. That'll be up to the Professor," came Mousey's meek response. "Sure thing."

Rocky jerked his head toward the door. "Let's scram. It's depressin' in here. Reminds me of stir."

With one final, sad, almost apologetic look at Dan, Mousey left the room. Rocky stared at Dan. "If you want anything, just ring for the butler."

The slamming of the door muffled Rocky's laugh. The sudden silence was punctuated only by Dan's own breathing and that annoying, steady drip of water somewhere in the gloom. For a moment, Dan lay still, as if by remaining motionless he might somehow convince himself this wasn't happening.

***

Paul stood frozen in place, his eyes fixed on the copperhead coiled just a few feet away. Its scales glistened under the dappled sunlight filtering through the trees, and its eyes met his with an unblinking, icy stare. The snake began to glide over the rustling leaves, each curve of its body moving in a seamless, hypnotic rhythm. A shiver traveled down Paul's spine, his mind racing with the realization that if he had dropped just a couple of inches to his left, he might have been within striking distance.

The snake slithered away. Paul watched until the last inch of its tail disappeared into the forest underbrush. Only then did Paul release a long, shaky breath, the sound escaping his lips like a balloon deflating. He turned his head in the direction Vic and Tommy had vanished, then scanned the other way.

Paul moved with care, placing each foot silently on the forest floor. Every few steps, he paused to listen, his senses heightened by fear and necessity. The woods breathed around him — leaves rustling, distant birds calling, the occasional scurry of small creatures in the brush. But no human voices. Not yet.

Minutes later, he stumbled out onto the old logging road.

The sudden openness made him feel exposed. Paul swiveled his head left, then right, scanning for any sign of movement. Only the empty road stretched away in both directions, its edges being reclaimed by nature bit by bit. No figures of Vic or Tommy. No human sound. Nothing. Just a safe silence.

He allowed himself a deep breath before breaking into a jog, heading toward the swamp. He was tired, but fear kept him moving. The vast expanse of dark water dotted with cypress trees and floating vegetation appeared around the next turn. Paul slowed, his eyes searching for any sign of the twins' canoe. He didn't see it.

"Dan?" Paul's voice was drowned out by the birds. Then louder: "Dan!"

The only reply to his call was the incessant buzzing of insects. The dock was empty. Dan must have reached it first and followed the instructions Paul had given him.

Paul knew he couldn't fault Dan for doing exactly what was asked of him. But even as he wrestled with the rightness of his own order, he couldn't help but feel a storm of anger and sadness that his twin had indeed left him behind. Yet, even as he stood there, torn between understanding and betrayal, he knew he had to decide his next move.

He was about to turn back to hide in the forest when something caught his eye — a flash of bright color against the murky water. Squinting, he made out their red cooler bobbing about twenty yards out. Beside it, their tarp floated like a blue island, and what looked like Dan's backpack drifted in a patch of duckweed.

Paul's stomach dropped. That didn't make any sense. Dan wouldn't toss out their gear willingly. He moved to the edge of the swamp. He spotted more debris — a paddle floating near a fallen tree, what might be their tent bag snagged on a branch that dipped into the water.

Where could Dan be? Paul's worry about his brother's safety grew. Had Dan escaped somehow? Did someone tamper with their canoe before Dan showed up? Maybe Dan discovered it and fled? But if he ran, where would he go? Or perhaps he heard Paul approaching, not knowing who it was, and decided to hide?

Then a worse thought hit him: Dan's body was submerged in the opaque water. The swamp could conceal a body for years.

A sudden, sharp snap of metal froze him mid-motion. The noise was crisp and unmistakable — a fracture in the forest's sounds that could only mean one thing. He stopped, going rigid as fear prickled through him, and spun around.

Vic and Tommy stood on the cracked, hard dirt of the deserted road. The polished surface of the gun in Vic's hand caught the light, reflecting a gleam that flashed like a warning signal. A slight breeze rustled the dry grass along the roadside. After a second, the two moved to Paul.

Tommy's face split into a triumphant grin. "Told you," he said to Vic, his voice dripping with satisfaction. "Told you he'd head for the water."

Vic nodded, his eyes never leaving Paul. "Smart play, kid. But not smart enough." They stopped in front of Paul. "End of the line now."

Paul's mind whirled as he mentally measured the distance to the nearest tree, estimated the angles of escape, and pondered every possible route. Behind him, the swamp spread out like a murky, stagnant moat. If he could just plunge far enough into the water and swim farther into the swamp...

"Don't even think about it," Vic warned. "You know what to do with your hands. Do it."

Paul slowly raised his hands. He felt something shift beneath his foot — a stone, smooth and round. His eyes flicked down to the ground, and his fingers twitched. One throw, one distraction might be all he needed.

"I wouldn't do that if I were you," Vic said, his voice dropping to a dangerous whisper. With his free hand, he reached into his coat pocket and brought out a short length of cord. "Here, Tommy. Tie his hands behind his back. In case he gets any other bright ideas."

"Yeah! You think we're stupid!" Tommy put in. He took a step closer, his movements deliberate, predatory. "I said, you think we're stupid? Huh? Just come with us nice and quiet like. The Professor will want a word with you."

Paul's hand stilled, the stone forgotten beneath his foot. His gaze moved between Vic's cold eyes and Tommy's eager ones, weighing his options. There weren't any. The swamp gurgled in back of him, a tempting, treacherous refuge, but now out of reach.

Tommy took the cord and moved closer. He approached Paul, turned him around, and pulled his hands behind his back. Paul grimaced as Tommy secured his wrists firmly. "I hope that hurts, punk." Once done, Tommy stepped in front of Paul, seized one arm, and spun him to face him and Vic. "Get going, pal."

"Get your hands off me," Paul spat back.

With a sneer, Tommy planted his palms on Paul's chest and gave him a hard shove, sending Paul stumbling backward until he stepped into the murky swamp. In retaliation, he kicked his leg powerfully, splashing a cascade of water toward Tommy. The droplets hit him square in the face, and he coughed, grimacing as he wiped his eyes with the back of his hand, muttering curses under his breath.

"Thought you could get away, huh?" Tommy sneered, his voice dripping with contempt. He jabbed his index finger at Paul. "You're gonna pay for that, pal."

Tommy lunged to grab Paul with both hands. Paul moved quickly, a fluid sidestep that left Tommy grasping at air and momentum. Paul hooked his foot around Tommy's ankle, a quick, precise motion that sent his opponent sprawling. Tommy hit the ground with a heavy thud, his face grinding into the mud.

Vic burst into laughter, the sound loud and mocking in the stillness. "Nice move, hothead. Outdone by a kid with his hands tied behind his back!" He laughed again.

Fury twisted Tommy's features as he scrambled to his feet, a dangerous fire in his eyes. "Nobody makes a fool of me. Nobody." His swords were not only a promise but a threat. He caught hold of Paul's shoulders and pushed him back to Vic. "Hold him."

Vic pinned Paul's arms. With a poisonous grin, Tommy threw a jab into Paul's stomach.

It was just the beginning. Tommy's fists were like unstoppable pistons, delivering a merciless barrage aimed at Paul's torso. Each punch crashed with a resounding thud, expelling the air from Paul's lungs and doubling him over in agony. The surrounding world dissolved into a chaotic blur, leaving only the excruciating sting of every blow, the brutal slap of skin smashing against skin. Paul's body convulsed with every impact, the pain coursing through him. Vic released Paul. He dropped to his knees, gasping.

"All right. That's enough, kid," Vic said, with the weary sound of a parent calling a child in from spending too much time outside playing.

The attack stopped, with Tommy's breathing coming in sharp pants, his fury radiating from him like waves of heat. He seized a fistful of Paul's hair, yanking his head upwards with a brutal pull. Leaning in, his breath was hot and foul as he spat in Paul's face, delivering the ultimate insult. He stepped back, his self-satisfied chuckle hanging in the thick, oppressive atmosphere.

"Get up," Vic said.

Paul pushed his body up from the ground. He rose in a series of unsteady movements, first getting on one knee, then the other, finally willing his legs to stand tall. He swayed slightly, his balance wavering as he took a moment to steady himself, trying to push away the waves of nausea. Tommy stood nearby, arms crossed and a mocking grin stretching across his face, enjoying Paul's struggle.

"This isn't finished," Paul said to Tommy.

Tommy gave a derisive snort. "Yeah, it is, pal. You have no idea how finished it is."

"Back to the mill," Vic said, jerking his head in its direction.

Chapter Eight

Dan twisted his wrists against the unyielding tape, the adhesive pulling at the fine hairs on his skin with each movement. He strained, muscles tensing as he tried to create even the smallest gap between his bound hands. Despite his efforts, the stuff instead seemed to grow tighter. His fingers, encased in their silver prison, felt numb and distant, as though they belonged to someone else entirely. He flexed them in desperation, seeking any weakness in Mousey's handiwork, but found none.

Rolling onto his side, Dan brought his knees toward his chest, thinking perhaps he could maneuver his hands past his feet and bring them in front of him. The effort sent fire shooting through his shoulders, his joints screaming in protest at the unnatural position. His ankles allowed for no more than an inch of separation. He persisted, rocking back and forth on the filthy concrete, his skin collecting more grime with each movement. Hopeless.

The adrenaline that had powered him during the chase faded away, leaving behind the ice-cold emptiness of fear. His thoughts turned to his mother, and how he regretted what he may be putting his mother through. She had already lost her husband to war; now he and maybe Paul could be gone, too.

No, Dan refused to think like that. That was useless. It wouldn't help. The twins weren't going anywhere. He and Paul have gotten out of nasty scrapes before. This would be another one they'd manage together. As one.

Dan lay still on the floor. The sour taste of the adhesive's chemical tang seeped through the gaps in the tape across his mouth. He closed his eyes, aware of the noises around him — the persistent drip of water counting seconds like a devilish metronome, the settling groans of the ancient mill, the skittering of unseen creatures in the dark corners.

Then, something new. Voices.

At first, Dan thought his mind had made them up. But the sounds grew clearer, more distinct. Footsteps coming down the stairs and shuffling along the basement floor outside, accompanied by the murmur of conversation. The sound stopped on the other side of the boiler room. The door swung open on protesting hinges.

A body stumbled through the doorway, propelled by a violent shove from behind. Vic, Tommy, and Rocky crowded the door, with Mousey peering in from in back of the group. Rocky held up the lantern. Paul turned to glare at Tommy.

"Quit your shoving," Paul said in a low, threatening voice.

"Yeah? Says who? You?" Tommy rang with cocky arrogance. He swaggered up to Paul and jabbed his finger into his chest. "You're going to be pushed around, get it?" Tommy slapped Paul. "And you're going to like it, get it?" Another slap.

Paul spotted Dan. In a single glance, an unspoken conversation passed between the twins: relief at seeing each other, anxiety about their predicament, and a resolute commitment to escape it. Dan tried to speak with his eyes, telling his brother not to fight. Paul understood and calmed down.

"Oh, Tommy," Vic said in a bored tone. "Stop talking like a cheap hood from the movies."

Tommy swaggered back to Rocky and jerked his thumb toward Paul. "What do we do with him?"

"That'll be up to the Professor," Rocky answered.

"And he won't just pat them on the head," Vic said. Tommy snickered.

"Until he gets here, let Mousey show off his new skill with tape. How about it, Mousey? Would you like that?" Rocky asked. Mousey looked up at Rocky and grinned, bobbing his head. Rocky pointed at Paul. "Okay. Do your stuff."

Mousey darted out of the room, returning with the roll of tape. He looked at the others, making sure they were watching, then strutted up to Paul like a bantam rooster. "I need his hands untied first."

"Do it, Tommy," Vic ordered.

Tommy looked sour at having to follow a command given by Mousey. He undid the cord binding Paul's wrists anyway, handing the rope back to Vic.

Mousey looked around and jerked his head at a corner of the room. "How about over there?" Rocky gave his approval with a nod. He spoke to Paul. "Sit by that pipe."

The pipe jutted up from the floor like an iron stalagmite. Paul's eyes flickered between Mousey and the others. He braced himself, moving his weight evenly onto his feet. Dan knew Paul was shifting into his boxing stance, figuring his chances of fighting his way out. Dan hoped his brother wouldn't try to break for it or fight. The gang would pulverize Paul if he tried to battle him. Paul glanced at Dan, and Dan gave a slight shake of his head.

"I said sit," Mousey repeated, his voice gaining confidence with every word. He waved the tape like a weapon.

Paul turned and moved slowly, each step deliberate as he crossed the gritty floor. Finally, he sat where told to.

Mousey's apparent self-assurance evaporated as he neared the glowering Paul with the caution of someone approaching a wild animal. He knelt behind Paul. "Don't move. Rocky doesn't like it when people move. Right, Rocky?"

"That's right, kid," Rocky said.

"Hands on either side of the pipe," Mousey instructed, tearing off a length of tape with his teeth. The sound — like fabric ripping — bounced around the room.

Paul hesitated, his jaw tightening.

"Now!" Rocky barked from the doorway.

Paul complied, stretching his arms back along the pipe.

Mousey began his work with the concentration of a surgeon. He threaded the tape between the pipe and Paul's wrists, creating a figure-eight pattern that secured his hands to the metal column.

"That's it, Mousey," Vic said from the door. "Nice and tight."

"Yeah. Make it hurt," Tommy chimed in.

Mousey nodded as layer upon layer of tape built around Paul's wrists. Paul winced as Mousey yanked particularly hard, forcing his shoulders to strain against the firm metal. Tommy chortled.

"The ankles now," Rocky said, stepping farther into the room. The lantern cast his enormous shadow on the far wall, a massive black specter that engulfed everything.

Mousey moved to Paul's feet, kneeling on the concrete. He positioned Paul's feet together.

"Don't move," Mousey murmured as he started to wrap tape around Paul's ankles. He worked with precision, ensuring each layer overlapped the one before by half. Once he finished, he leaned back on his knees, tore off two more strips of tape, and placed them over Paul's mouth. "How's that, Rocky?"

Rocky nodded in approval. "Very good, kid."

Mousey stood beaming.

"What about the other one?" Vic jerked his head at Dan. "He shouldn't be loose like that."

"Yeah, you're right about that, Vic." Rocky rubbed the back of his head with one meaty hand.

"How about that pipe over there?" Mousey pointed to one on the opposite side of the boiler from Paul.

"That's using your head, Mousey. Alright, get him up." Rocky gestured at Dan.

Mousey reached for Dan, slipping his hands under Dan's arms. He began to drag him toward the pipe that angled up from one that came from the boiler, snapped off halfway to the ceiling. Despite Dan being larger and heavier, Mousey managed to pull him along the floor, grunting at the effort. Dan's muscles, already tense from resting on the chilly concrete, ached.

"Come on, keep moving!" Mousey's voice was tinged with nervous energy as he tugged Dan along the concrete.

An old bottle — perhaps once containing some long-forgotten maintenance fluid — lay in the path. Mousey's face contorted with sudden, out-of-place rage at this minor obstacle. He lashed out with his foot, connecting with the bottle and sending it spinning across the ground. It struck the boiler with a hollow, musical clang.

"Stupid thing," Mousey said, as if the bottle had placed itself in his way on purpose. The flare-up pleased Tommy, who chuckled from the doorway.

At last, they reached the pipe. Mousey paused, stepped over Dan, and then bent down to get a better grip. "Fight back!" he said to Dan in a quiet voice.

It was an odd command, leaving Dan wondering what was going on. Was Mousey trying to help him, possibly out of gratitude for standing up to Rocky on the kid's behalf? Or was it to show off to the gang? Or something else? Dan had no idea, but decided to obey anyway. He put up a struggle.

"Stop it!" Mousey stood with his back to the group, blocking Dan from their view. He pretended to launch a brutal kick at Dan's side. Dan, going along with the act, let out a cry, still unsure of the reason for the charade. The gang thought it was real and laughed.

"That's right, Mousey!" Tommy applauded. "Show him who's boss, little man!"

Mousey got on his knees and wrapped his arms around Dan in a bear hug. He put his lips next to Dan's ear and whispered. "This pipe is almost rusted through."

He hoisted Dan, placing his back against the cold metal. The pipe's surface was uneven beneath Dan's bare skin, ridged with flaking rust and scratchy insulation that crumbled at contact. Mousey released his grip on Dan and stepped back, surveying his work-in-progress.

With a satisfied nod, Mousey tore off a long strip with his teeth. He pressed the adhesive onto the middle of Dan's torso, wrapping it twice around both Dan and the pipe.

"More," Rocky said. "I want him to be part of that pipe."

"Okay, Rocky." Mousey nodded as he ripped off another length, this one going across Dan's chest and around the pipe. Mousey's nimble fingers smoothed down each additional layer, ensuring no wrinkles or air bubbles that might create weakness. The last piece wrapped around Dan's stomach, securing him to the pipe in three places.

Mousey got up and faced Rocky. He waved a hand toward Dan. "There! How's that? See? He ain't going nowhere! And he can fight all he wants!"

"Good! We'll make a man out of you yet, Mousey!" Rocky checked his watch. "We have some time. Let's run a batch of tens. The Professor should be comin' soon, and he likes seein' us busy."

"I oiled the press real good and installed that new roller." Mousey bubbled with excitement. "She'll run real smooth! Just you wait and see!"

"You and machines," Vic said with a chuckle.

Mousey looked back at Dan. Dan thought he detected a glint of encouragement flashing from the kid's eyes.

With Mousey leading the way, Vic and Tommy left the room. Rocky held up the lantern to take one more look at Dan and Paul. He shook his head. "It's too bad you found us, boys."

He shut the door. The blackness of the boiler room surrounded the brothers and pressed on Dan's eyes until odd, ghostly forms danced before him. Paul put in a desperate fight against his restraints, the frantic movements coming through the dark. His breath became ragged and erratic, filled with either fear or pain. In a few minutes, the struggle stopped. Paul must have given up.

The atmosphere in the room was muggy and stifling. The constant drip-drip-drip of water reverberated around them, like the water torture Dan had heard of. Each drop marked the time Dan dreaded was slipping away.

Dan's thoughts drifted back to the last words Mousey had said to him: "The pipe is almost rusted through." What did that mean? Why did he tell him that?

Mousey suggested to Rocky the pipe to bind Dan to. Did the younger boy have a plan? A way to help Dan escape? If so, was it really enough? Would it work? But the thought of possibly freeing himself offered a faint bit of hope to Dan. He wanted to trust Mousey, but could he? He was one of the gang, after all. But then again, he may have to believe him anyway. It could be the twins' only way out...

Dan's fingertips probed the ground behind him, coming across rust flakes, sharp and brittle. He wondered if this fragile debris did point the way to freedom. Now to figure out how all the pieces went together, so he could understand what Mousey was hinting to him.

He was bound to a pipe, which tilted upward from a right-angle joint. The bottom connected to a larger one that disappeared into the ancient boiler's underbelly. The cast-iron pipe — that's what it must be, given the age of the mill — had a rough texture beneath his exploring fingers.

Dan remembered a plumber doing work at their house once, cursing the brittleness of old cast iron, how it would eventually rot from the interior, maintaining its shape while losing its strength, becoming a hollow shell of its former self.

"The older it gets," the plumber complained, "the more it turns to glass inside. One good shock and —" He'd snapped his fingers for emphasis.

Decades of steam, condensation and rust may have worked their slow, destructive progress on the pipe at Dan's back, he realized. Cast iron didn't bend when it failed; it shattered, broke apart in jagged shards and razor edges.

As Dan adjusted his position, more flakes of rust sprinkled down, and the pipe creaked under the strain — a soft, disapproving moan. This was a good sign. The metal may be weak and could break. But how to do that? Even if he had a hammer handy, there was no way he handle it.

Three courses of tape bound him to the pipe. Perhaps that was a clue to Mousey's plan. The weird command to "struggle" allowed Mousey willingly to follow Rocky's order to make Dan "part of the pipe." So by using the three strips of tape, Mousey lashed Dan in a way that gave him more leverage; the pipe was less likely to slip when moved. So even if he couldn't whack the cast iron, perhaps he could wiggle it... like a loose tooth.

Dan hesitated, then he pushed backward. The corroded metal pipe's roughness bit through into his skin. A deep, resonant groan came from the old cast iron, more pronounced than before. He stopped, wondering if the noise would be detected. Then he heard something from upstairs.

Clack-clack-thump. Clack-clack-thump.

The gang had started the printing press. Good. That would drown out any sounds Dan made down here.

He adjusted his position to sit up straight against the pipe as he was able, then started shifting his weight first to the left, then to the right. Side to side, side to side, creating a deliberate swaying pattern that mimicked the rhythmic drip of water echoing through the space. With each move, the jagged metal surface scraped along his spine, sending a shiver through him.

Left and right... left and right... left and right...

Clack-clack-thump. Clack-clack-thump.

It was harder work than he had thought. Sweat gathered on his forehead, forming tiny beads that slid down his temples, carving trails through the dust on his skin. A single droplet hesitated at the tip of his nose before gravity claimed it, sending it to merge with the growing puddle in his lap. The sharp sting of salt in his eyes blurred his vision, but he blinked it away, his mind zeroing in on the job at hand.

At first, it seemed like nothing was happening, and Dan was wasting his effort. But soon, the pipe appeared to become a bit more unstable. It was a subtle yet clear change.

Dan caught his breath before resuming his efforts. The pipe groaned once more, this time emitting a higher-pitched sound, reminiscent of metal nearing its limit. In his mind, Dan repeated to himself, "This might work, this might work."

Left and right... left and right... left and right...

Clack-clack-thump. Clack-clack-thump.

His shoulders ached with the strain, his muscles knotting as he pushed harder against the resistance. Beads of sweat trickled down his chest and spine. Strands of hair stuck to his forehead, slick and darkened by the perspiration.

The pipe wiggled and wobbled behind Dan's back. With every sideways movement, Dan's swaying grew more and more, his body shifting back and forth in wider arcs as he pushed the ancient cast iron to its failure point.

He rested, gasping for breath in the soupy air. He was exhausted, but knew he couldn't stop. Breathing deeply, Dan resumed his

efforts with renewed energy, grunting as he threw his weight —
left, right, left, right — despite all his muscles screaming in protest.
But as he continued, he felt the pipe weaken more and more, as he
heard the crunch of oxidized metal giving way beneath his assault.

The pipe gave a final, eerie groan, like some dying beast, before
giving way. The fragile cast iron broke apart, causing Dan to pitch
onto the concrete floor on his side. He inhaled sharply as pain
radiated through his side from the impact. A piece of pipe was still
attached to his back, held by duct tape, even though the original
attachment had given out.

A muffled voice came from Paul. It almost sounded like "Dan?"

"OK," Dan grunted back.

He lay still for several seconds. He was now a bizarre hu-
man-pipe creation, like some industrial tortoise. The weight of
the pipe — perhaps two feet long and six inches in diameter —
weighed uncomfortably against his shoulder blades. But he was
free — sort of.

Dan turned onto his stomach. His hands, still tied behind him,
were now sandwiched between his back and the rounded surface of
the pipe, making his position even more uncomfortable. He now
realized he hadn't planned his next move after breaking free. With
his ankles bound together and the pipe on his back, he couldn't
hop anywhere. After some thought, he decided to inch his way
over to Paul. Maybe his brother had better use of his fingers and
could work on peeling the tape binding Dan's hands.

But the awkward metal appendage taped to his back made
simple movement difficult. Dan couldn't afford to have the pipe

clanking and scraping against the floor, announcing every change of his position like a blaring trumpet. That left one way he could think of. He started to slither, snake-like, toward Paul.

The press stopped upstairs, replaced with the sound of voices in conversation. Dan froze. Did that mean the gang had finished printing the bills, or did that mean —

The door at the top of the basement stairs creaked open. Rocky's voice cracked through the air like a thunderbolt. "They're down in the boiler room."

A second voice — mellow, rich, cultured, speaking with a French accent — answered.

"You say there are two of them?"

"Yes, Professor," Rocky replied.

The Professor had arrived. Footsteps started down the steps.

Panic gripped Dan. Rocky couldn't discover him in the middle of the floor, on the loose. He had to return to where he was and try to make it appear that he was still tied to a rigid pipe. And he had to do it before Rocky and the Professor stepped into the boiler room.

Chapter Nine

The voices grew louder with each step down the stairs, matching each thud of Dan's pulse pounding in his ears. His heart raced, adrenaline coursing through his veins like wildfire, making him lightheaded.

Dan began a retreat to his original position. The rough, cold texture of the concrete floor chafed against his bare chest and stomach as he inched, slithered, and wiggled his way backward. To him, every one of his movements boomed through in the darkened room, every shuffle and breath magnified as if being broadcast over the radio.

The French voice continued, closer now. "They will keep for a moment. Tell me, how are the shipments proceeding?"

Rocky and the Professor seemed to pause near the table, talking about how to get rid of the fake money. At least that bought Dan some extra time.

He made it back to his starting point, his head connecting with the jagged edge of the rusted pipe jutting out from the awkward right-angle joint. Now he needed to sit up and make the two parts of the broken piece appear as one. With his hands bound, and the pipe segment tapped to his back like the fin of a prehistoric beast, each movement was a battle.

Twisting his torso, he gritted his teeth as he shifted himself to where he was when he began. After a couple of clumsy attempts, grunting with the effort, he rolled to a sitting position. He scooted backward on his rear, inch by inch, until he was in front of the snapped pipe.

Beads of perspiration trickled down his forehead, mingling with the dust and grime on his skin, as he tried to align the broken piece with its original connection, his muscles taut and trembling with the exertion.

But the section on his back refused to cooperate. All his movements on the floor must have shifted it somewhat, and he felt it tilting at an awkward angle. It would be obvious that the pipe was not whole.

Sweat poured into Dan's eyes, burning and blurring his vision. He blinked rapidly, trying to clear his sight while adjusting his posture. The tape around his wrists had begun to soften in the heat and moisture, giving a bit when he strained against it, but not enough to free him.

"Okay, Professor," Rocky said as he and the mysterious head of the gang finished their discussion by the table. "They're in here."

Dan made a final adjustment, sitting up at an uncomfortable angle to compensate for the slipped pipe, straining to hold the broken pieces in a position that might, in poor lighting, appear as one. He forced his breathing to slow, so his breath won't jiggle the loose pipe. He lowered his chin to his chest, allowing his sweat-soaked hair to fall forward, partially covering his forehead. The doorknob rattled.

Dan took a deep breath and held his head up, hoping that would help the illusion. The door swung open with a long creak. Rocky stepped into the room, holding the lantern high. Dan remained motionless, his muscles trembling with the effort of maintaining the awkward pose. The pipe segment shifted a slight bit, and he pressed harder against it, willing the metal to remain still.

The Professor strode into the room. His height and slender frame accentuated the sophistication of his navy pin-striped suit, complemented by a powder blue shirt. A maroon tie, perfectly knotted, added a bold touch, while a fresh white carnation nestled in his lapel. His thinning black hair, meticulously combed back, highlighted his sharp features. Above his upper lip rested a precisely groomed pencil-thin mustache, completing his distinguished appearance. He clasped his long, delicate fingers in front of him as he glanced between the brothers.

"My! They are like... what is the expression? 'Two peas in a pod?'" the Professor asked. His black eyes looked through Dan, not at him.

"Yeah, that's it," Rocky said.

"And they saw..." the Professor prompted.

"Everything. The press, the money, everything," Rocky said.

"How unfortunate for them." The Professor clucked his tongue. "However, it does confirm my decision. There is a more important matter to tend to first."

Rocky reacted with a start. "More important? What's that?"

"The foolish passer in this area grew greedy and distributed too much of our product around in one place," the Professor said. "That aroused the interest of the American government, which flooded the region with Treasury agents. We must clear out of here at once to another headquarters in a neighboring state. I have acquired a new property."

"You mean move everything?" Rocky sputtered in disbelief.

"That is correct."

"But we spent months findin' this joint and settin' it up!" Rocky protested.

"If these two found it, others may do as well," the Professor replied.

"It was luck!" Rocky said.

The Professor gave a derisive chuckle. "Some luck. But it represents possible discovery by additional parties. This was an excellent location, but now we must change to be cautious."

"But it'll take hours just to break down and move the press alone," Rocky said. "Listen, I think we —"

The Professor interrupted Rocky with an icy stare. He spoke with an undercurrent of unmistakable threat. "You will continue to take orders, will you not, Rocky?"

The enormous man shrank back. "Yes... Yes, Professor. Yes, I will," Rocky at last fumbled out.

"That is a wise decision." The Professor took a sniff of his carnation. "We need to remove any traces of our occupation here. All of them. That, of course, will include these two." He gave a dismissive wave toward the twins.

"What do you want us to do with them?"

"Whatever it is, it cannot appear to be foul play," the Professor said. "There may be others — families, friends — who would search for them when they don't return. If the police find these two with marks that do not indicate an accident, they will search the area more thoroughly. That would complicate our operation."

"What do you have in mind?" Rocky asked.

"You said they came in a canoe?"

Rocky nodded. "Yeah. We sank it."

"Bon." The Professor cast another sweeping wave of his hand over Dan and Paul. "And our guests are wearing bathing costumes. The answer is simple, no? It is there in front of us. When we finish cleaning up here, we take them to the water and drown them. Then we release their bodies into the river. Thus, they become another sad, fatal, summer swimming accident."

A chill and a shiver ran through Dan. He stiffened again, trying to keep the illusion that the broken pipe wasn't.

"Yeah, okay. That'll work," Rocky nodded.

"Now we will return to the others and get ready to 'roll up our cuffs,'" the Professor said.

"Sleeves. The expression is 'roll up our sleeves,'" Rocky corrected.

"Ah, yes! 'Roll up our sleeves.' The English language... it is most difficult," the Professor said with a slight shrug of his shoulders.

They left the room, shutting the door behind them. As soon as it clicked closed, Dan let out a shaky breath, his chest aching from the strain of staying motionless. The Professor's unemotional voice echoed in his memory, detailing the grim future planned for him and his brother.

Drowning. The plan was to drown them. The way the Professor said the word was both terrifying and disturbingly clinical.

Dan's brain bounced between panic and determination. He decided that the Professor's idea would not be the brothers' fate. But doubt crept in — what could he do to really prevent it?

Then Dan grew angry. The Professor's plan would not happen. At least not without a fight. Rocky said disassembling and moving the printing press would take hours. Good. That would occupy the gang, so none of them would come back down here to check on the brothers. Maybe.

He went back to his original plan. Dan needed to make his way across the boiler room to reach Paul once more and see if his twin had enough hand movement to loosen Dan's bonds.

Dan dropped to his side again. It was as unpleasant as the first time. He rolled onto his stomach, grimacing as the rough concrete dug into his already raw skin from his earlier trips along the floor. But he still had to move.

He began to crawl, or rather, to slither forward in a strange, sinuous motion. He could only propel himself by digging his toes into the cement and pushing. At the same time, he twisted, hunched, and unhunched his shoulders to inch ahead.

The steady drip of water came monotonously through the dark room, every droplet creating a rhythmic splash as it hit the ground. Dan's eyes seemed to twitch with each plunk, the ticking of a clock reverberating in his skull, beating a silent warning: time was slipping away.

The pipe piece strapped to Dan's back wobbled when he moved, its weight sometimes pulling him off balance and risking a loud clang on the floor. Each time that happened, he halted, holding his breath as if the gang might hear him despite the door being shut.

A muffled sound from Paul broke the silence — a low, guttural grunt or maybe an angry word smothered by a gag. It cut through the darkness like a beacon, providing Dan with a sense of direction amid the disorienting blackness to the pipe Paul was tied to. He focused on the source of the noise and made his way toward it.

From above came the sound of the gang's activity. Cardboard boxes were dragged across the floor with a dull scrape, feet shuffled rhythmically in unison, and the sharp metallic clatter of pieces of the printing press being taken apart blended together... punctuated by the occasional, loud curse.

Dan's determined crawl came to an abrupt stop when his head bumped into something soft: his brother's leg. Adjusting his position, Dan shifted himself to lie alongside his brother, his left shoulder touching Paul's leg. Dan started forward again, keeping contact with his twin. At last, his shoulder rubbed against Paul's hip.

Paul moved his fingers, wiggling them. Gentle taps came on Dan's shoulder, giving him an idea of where he was in relation to his brother's hands. Dan continued his awkward forward motion. The tapping continued, tracing a path down Dan until Paul's fingers brushed against Dan's waist, near where the duct tape secured his hands.

Dan adjusted his position on the hard floor, trying to get as close to his brother as possible. Paul's fingers trembled as they slid between the pipe and Dan's back, reaching for the tape around Dan's wrists. Despite Dan twisting his body in ways he never imagined he could, Paul couldn't get a solid hold on the tape. His fingers kept slipping off the slick surface.

"Uh-uh," Paul said through his gag.

Dan lay back on the ground, letting out a frustrated moan. He racked his brain. Okay, that didn't work. If Dan couldn't use his hands... how about his teeth?

He backed up, sliding along Paul's side until his face was close to Paul's hands. He leaned in, pressing the tape gag against Paul's fingers. "My mouth. My mouth." With luck, what he came out sounding like the actual words.

Paul got it. His fingers searched for the edge of the tape covering Dan's mouth. After some fumbling, he snagged a corner with his fingertips. He said something like, "Okay."

With a series of quick, forceful jerks, Dan pulled his head back. The adhesive stretched and peeled away from his skin. The gag tore off, a sharp sting spreading across his raw, reddened lips.

"Ow," Dan said quietly. "Okay, buddy, no gag. I'm going to try to tear through the tape around your hands with my teeth."

Dan contorted himself again, shifting onto his side on the hard floor, the rough surface pressing against his ribs. He pushed his face forward until his nose touched Paul's hand. Opening his mouth wide, he clamped his teeth down on the tough, gray duct tape that held Paul's wrist to the metal pipe. Dan attacked it, twisting his neck at awkward angles while he gnawed and tugged at the stubborn adhesive.

The tape was just as determined to remain attached, sticky and strong. After several intense minutes of chewing and tearing, his mouth sore and his breath heavy, Dan let go of his grip. He pulled back, wanting to see if he had made any progress.

"Try freeing your hands," Dan urged.

"Uh-uh," came from Paul after a few seconds of struggle.

Dan bared his teeth again as he clamped down again onto the edge of the tape, biting down with the ferocity of a desperate, starving rat. His jaw muscles strained under the pressure, and a dull, persistent ache pulsed through his cheeks, radiating up to his temples with every twist. The sticky taste of adhesive coated his tongue. He released his bite, panting as he drew back.

"Now?" Dan asked.

Paul's response after some tugging at the binding was a resigned "no."

What now? Dan let his head fall to the ground, his thoughts in a tangled mess. He needed a plan, but nothing came to mind that seemed possible. Perhaps the twins could find a chance to try for an escape when the gang took them to the water, but was that realistic? Two against five?

From upstairs, the clatter of metal continued as the dismantling of the printing press continued piece by piece. Footsteps crossed the floorboards above, and cardboard boxes rustled as they stuffed papers and equipment inside. Rocky's gruff voice sliced through the chaos, barking orders with a razor-sharp edge. Dan imagined the Professor sitting back, sniffing his carnation perhaps, supervising the entire process.

"Careful with that!" Rocky shouted as someone dropped something on the floor that shattered. Most likely, it must have been a...

A bottle! Dan's head popped up. An idea occurred to him, but not the means to carry it out. Dan recalled that Mousey had kicked a bottle out of the way while he was dragging Dan over to the pipe.

How could he have forgotten that! Glass! He could use the edges of broken glass as a knife! For that, he needed the bottle. The question was, where did it end up? And could he find it in the darkness?

"I think I've got something," Dan said to Paul.

Dan remembered the sharp clink the glass made when it struck the boiler. With any luck, it didn't ricochet and roll farther away into the darkness once it hit. The location he needed to reach should be somewhere on his right.

Resuming his awkward, snake-like slide on his belly, Dan wriggled toward his goal. How far away was that thing? He was certain he'd already gone all the way to Chicago. After a few minutes, he wondered if he had overshot his target.

The cold metal of the boiler grazed his shoulder, causing him to stop. "Didn't reach Chicago. Bingo!" he said to himself. He nudged around the base of the furnace with his nose, much like a blind pig searching through dense underbrush for the elusive prize of a hidden corncob.

A soft clinking sound reached his ears, and a sensation on his nose signaled he had found his target. He explored a little more with his nose. The bottle lay next to the boiler, its glass neck angled towards him but off straight on.

Dan opened his mouth and tried to grasp the neck of the bottle with his teeth. His first try was unsuccessful; his bite slipped, causing the bottle to wobble precariously before rolling gently out of his immediate grasp.

Adjusting his approach, he made another attempt. He tilted his head to the side, parting his lips slightly as he edged closer to his target. His lips touched the glass again. The angle still felt awkward.

He extended his tongue and used it to nudge the bottle ever so little until it moved, settling into a better position. He clamped his teeth down firmly around the neck of the bottle, securing it with a tight grip.

Now for part two. He lifted his head, listening to the noise from the room overhead. As soon as he heard loud clanking sounds start, Dan quickly reared his head higher, the bottle in his mouth. He jerked his head down and shut his eyes, smashing the glass onto the hard concrete floor.

It didn't break. With a frustrated growl, he lifted the bottle again and gave one more try to bash it on the floor. The glass remained as whole on the second try as on the first.

Just his luck, Dan thought. He got the world's only bottle made of unbreakable glass.

On the third attempt, he used all the force he could manage as he brought the bottle down. A sharp crack echoed through the room as the glass finally broke.

He couldn't see the result. Setting his handiwork down on the ground with a soft clink, he opened his lips. He stretched out his neck, stuck out his tongue, and gingerly prodded the edge of the broken glass. It met with jagged shards still attached to the neck. He had managed to break it right, creating a crude, improvised blade. He hoped.

So now all he had to do was maneuver back to his brother, carrying his makeshift knife in his mouth. Next, he had to cut the duct tape that tied Paul's hands to the pipe — without slicing Paul to pieces in the process. Then free him before the gang completed their packing and proceeded with their plan to take the twins to the swamp and drown them.

"Easy. Duck soup," Dan said under his breath. "Paul, I'm coming," he said, his voice low and hoarse.

He clamped the bottleneck in his mouth.

Chapter Ten

D an wriggled across the uneven concrete, heading back to his brother, the pipe on his back fused to him like a metal spine. Loud metallic clangs and grunts came from overhead as the gang continued to pack and move their equipment.

Reaching Paul, Dan set the bottle down; its clink on the floor tinkled like a tiny bell. "Alright, I'm going to cut you loose with a piece of glass. I'll try not to slice you up. Let me know if the glass touches your skin. Okay?"

Paul's muffled response sounded like "ot-ay."

"Sit as still as you can. Hang on, I'm going to start." Dan inhaled deeply and gripped the jagged bottle with his teeth. He guided the sharp edge towards the pipe, sliding it down until it stopped. He prayed it rested on a bundle of tape and not Paul's hand. "Eddy?" he asked with his created knife in his mouth, hoping it resembled "ready".

"Uh-huh," Paul answered.

Dan started to saw the jagged, broken glass against the tape. He moved his head back and forth, back and forth. The adhesive was strong, fighting his efforts. He gritted his teeth, applying more pressure, forcing the bottle's edge to dig into the tape. Paul winced, a sharp, muffled gasp escaping his lips as the glass nicked his skin. Dan sensed Paul's muscles tense, every fiber in his body coiled tightly, like a spring on the verge of snapping.

"Okay?" Dan said.

"Uh-huh."

Dan returned to his task, each movement as precise as he could make it. The jagged shard started to win the battle as the duct tape began to give way bit by bit, its fibers fraying. He worked the bottle, drawing it forward and back, forward and back, in a steady rhythm. Paul adjusted his position, a small shift that offered Dan the idea that his work was succeeding.

His breath hitched in quick, uneven gasps as Dan continued. He was getting tired, and it weighed him down like lead. It seemed as though he had been at this task forever, each minute seeming like hours. The duct tape slackened again, and Dan paused his slicing. "Try again," he said to his brother.

Paul fought to loosen his hand. "Uh-uh. More."

The rhythmic scrape of glass on tape resumed, sawing motions punctuated by Dan's labored breathing. The bottleneck, slick and dripping with his saliva, cut deeper. As more fibers frayed and parted, the sticky binding yielded to the persistence of the emergency knife.

"Go," Dan said.

Paul struggled with his bonds, and all at once his hand broke loose and flew out, striking Dan's head. Soon, the sound of tape being ripped off filled the air as Paul attacked the rest of the tape.

"That takes care of the gag," Paul said quietly. "Let me have that cutter."

Dan put it on the floor. He also kept his voice down. "By my head. Next to your hip."

Paul's hand probed around Dan's face until it grabbed the bottle. "Ew. It's covered with slobber."

"Well, excuse me," Dan returned.

"Not to worry," Paul said. After a short pause, accompanied by some grunting, he added, "I've freed my other hand. Time to work on the ankles." The sounds of tape being cut and torn came through the darkness. "Alright, it's your turn now, buddy."

Paul knelt beside Dan, his movements careful in the dark. He tapped the pipe. "What's this?"

"That's what Mousey tied me to," Dan answered. "It was rusted, so I broke it free."

Paul was incredulous. "You've been doing all this with that thing attached to you?"

"Yeah."

Paul gripped Dan's shoulder and squeezed it. "What a plumber you'd make, my dear brother."

Dan grinned. "Thanks."

"Hold still. This may hurt a little." Dan's fingers worked methodically around the pipe, seeking the edges of the tape that bound it to Dan's back. Every tug made Dan grimace as the adhesive was cut and yanked off him.

"Sorry," Paul whispered. "I'll try to take it a little easier."

"That's okay," Dan mumbled into the concrete. "Just get that stupid thing off me."

The tape peeled away with a sound like skin being stripped off, and felt like it. Dan shuddered, clamping his mouth shut to stifle any short yelps of pain. As Paul worked, Dan's lungs expanded more with each strip removed, the pressure gradually lessening across his shoulder blades.

"Almost done. Ride it out, buddy," Paul said, his voice tight with concentration. "Wow, this thing is really stuck to you."

With a final, decisive pull, the pipe came free. Dan gasped as air rushed against his sweaty back, while Paul set the pipe aside as softly as he could. The sudden absence of weight made Dan feel as though he might float away like a helium balloon.

"Man, that's a relief," Dan breathed, rolling his shoulders.

"Now for your hands."

Dan's wrists had gone numb long ago, the circulation cut off by layers of gray tape wrapped as tightly as it was. Paul worked the jagged bottle edge carefully between Dan's hands, cutting back and forth.

"How are your fingers? Can you feel them?" Paul asked in a low voice.

"Not really," Dan said. "Just pins and needles."

The tape on his wrists at last gave way, and Dan's arms fell limply to his sides. Pain shot through his shoulders as blood rushed back into his hands, thousands of prickings beneath his skin.

"Ankles next," Paul said, moving down to Dan's feet.

The tape around Dan's ankles had been applied with fewer layers, and Paul made quick work of it. As the final restraint dropped away, Dan lay still for a moment, savoring the sensation of being unbound and able to move freely again. It was a simple pleasure he'd never thought to appreciate before.

Paul helped Dan to sit up. "Can you stand?"

Dan nodded, flexing his fingers. "Yeah. Give me a minute for my plasma to make a lap."

Paul clamped a hand on Dan's back and gave his twin an affectionate pat. "My dear brother, you're the best."

"And you're not half-bad yourself," Dan grinned.

Paul removed the final pieces of tape from Dan's chest and stomach that had secured the pipe to his back. Dan winced at the sharp sting. Paul wadded up the sticky stuff and tossed it to the ground.

With a deep breath, Dan climbed to his feet, swaying a bit as blood rushed to his limbs. His legs tingled, making him grimace. He flexed his toes inside his shoes, willing sensation to return.

"Are you alright?" Paul stood by his brother, gripping him by his arms.

Dan nodded, then spoke. "Yeah. We need to move before they come back."

The sound of a heavy object being dragged upstairs toward the outside door, accompanied by grunting, came from above them. Shuffling footsteps crossed the floor, at times interrupted by a curse.

"The door should be that way," Paul said. He added in a grumble, "One thing was for darn certain, I didn't just graduate from high school only to be drowned in a swamp by a bunch of crooks. Especially not a fancy pants one with a French accent."

Taking Dan by the arm, Paul headed through the darkness, aiming for the door. They moved with caution, each step calculated to make as little noise as possible. "Here it is." Paul's hand shot out to stop Dan's progress.

Voices grew louder as somebody descended the stairs. The brothers froze, their backs pressed against the wall, hardly breathing.

"I don't believe this," Tommy grumbled. "Moving all of this! And we do all the heavy lifting while the Professor just sits there and gives orders."

"Keep your voice down," Vic said sharply. "You want him to overhear you?"

"I don't care if he does," Tommy retorted, though his volume noticeably lowered.

"You'd better care, pal," Vic said. "Remember what happened to Washington when he mouthed off? It wasn't pretty."

There was a pause. "No, it wasn't," Tommy said.

"So shut your trap and help me with these bills," Vic said. "We need to pack this up and take it to the truck."

The rustle of paper and the slap of stacks being moved came from the other side of the door.

"The Professor might be crazy, but he knows his stuff. This is quality work. I gotta hand it to him." Vic's admiration was clear in his tone. "You know, he told me he worked with the Germans during the war on a plan to flood England with fake money."

"Bully for him. Still doesn't mean I have to like him," Tommy spat out.

"Do you want to go challenge him, big man?" Vic challenged, his voice sharp.

A moment of silence came before Tommy answered, "No."

"That's using your head," Vic said. "Now, help me with these boxes."

"Wait. Where's my soda?" Tommy said. "Got it. Come on."

The wooden steps creaked as Vic and Tommy hauled the heavy load upstairs, their shoes thudding with each step. The muted rustle of cardboard against their shirts and the occasional grunt of effort filled the air. A hush soon settled over the building.

Paul put his mouth next to Dan's ear. "Why is it so quiet all of a sudden up top? It's creepy."

"It could be they're carrying stuff to their truck," Dan answered. He applied gentle pressure to the handle, terrified it might squeak, and cracked open the door, unsure of what they would find on the other side.

The space was empty other than the table, the stacks of counterfeit bills and boxes they'd glimpsed earlier gone. Paul stepped out first, his shoes scraping against the gritty floor. He gestured for Dan to follow, pressing a finger to his lips.

"They all could be outside, but we can't be sure." Dan scanned the room and pointed to the angled cellar doors that led out. Freedom was just a short dash away.

They moved cautiously across the basement, not knowing where the rest of the gang was, with Paul taking the lead. They had almost made it to the steps when voices from the hall stopped them.

"We need to check that we've taken everything from downstairs," Rocky, gruff and impatient, said to someone. "The Professor will skin us alive if we leave anything behind."

"But I already checked twice," came Mousey's whining reply. "It's clean."

"Well, check it again," Rocky barked. "I'll help. The truck's loaded."

Footsteps crossed the floor upstairs, growing louder. Coming toward the basement door.

Dan's eyes widened. He grabbed Paul's arm, yanking him backward. They retreated, moving as fast as silence would allow, heading back to the boiler room. Their only sanctuary.

They slipped back inside just as Rocky's heavy boots clumped on the top cellar step. Paul closed the door behind them with agonizing slowness, careful not to let the latch click. The two put their backs against the wall, shoulder to shoulder. Through the door, they heard Rocky and Mousey coming into the basement.

"See? Nothing here," Mousey said. "Vic and Tommy got everything."

Rocky grunted a reply.

Footsteps — lighter, softer — moved closer to where the brothers hid. The doorknob turned, metal scraping against metal.

Dan's eyes darted around the darkened room. There was nowhere to hide — just the boiler, pipes, and the concrete floor where they'd been held captive. The pipe he'd been bound to lay in plain sight, surrounded by torn duct tape. Evidence of their escape was scattered across the ground like a neon sign. Dan felt Paul tensing his muscles, ready to spring on anybody coming into the room.

"Where do you think you're goin'?" Rocky's sharp voice cut in.

The doorknob stopped turning. Mousey responded, hesitant. "I was gonna check on the two guys. You know, see if they want anything, like a drink of water."

Rocky roared, "What do you think this place is, a hotel? Leave 'em. Besides, they'll get plenty of water when we drown them." His laughter bounced through the basement, a rough, grating sound that sent ice through Dan's veins. "Come on, let's see if there's more to do upstairs."

The pair of footsteps retreated, followed by the basement door closing. Silence descended, broken only by the brothers' shallow breathing.

Dan swallowed. "We've got to make tracks. Now."

Paul pressed his ear against the door. After a moment, he eased it open a crack. The area was empty. The cellar doors at the opposite end still represented their best chance at escape.

"Ready?" Paul whispered.

Dan nodded. "Let's go."

They slipped out of the boiler room. Dan winced as his shoe scuffed on the floor. How could the gang not hear that? How could anybody on the planet not? The brothers must sound like a marching band made up of hippopotamus.

The two made their way to the steps leading to the exterior double cellar doors. Dan reached them first, his hands trembling as he pressed his palms on the rough wooden surface. He pushed gently at first, then with increasing force. The doors didn't budge.

"They're locked," Dan whispered. He ran his fingers along the seam where the doors met, searching for a lock mechanism. "The gang must have latched them from the outside."

They stood in silence for a moment. Inches separated them from freedom, yet they were still trapped. Rocky and Mousey's voices upstairs were more distant, but occasional thumps and footsteps reminded them that at least two of their captors were still in the building.

"What now?" Paul glanced around the basement. His eyes fell on the small window near the ceiling. It was narrow — barely a foot high and maybe two feet wide — but it might be their only chance. He pointed. "We could try that."

Dan followed his gaze. His voice was full of doubt. "It's pretty tiny. Mousey could get through, but us..."

"Yeah, we're bigger than him," Paul said. "But if we can get it open, I think we can squeeze through."

They moved quickly under the window. What was left of the glass was webbed with cracks and coated with decades of dust, making it impossible to see what lay beyond. Paul looked for something to stand on and spotted an old wooden crate in the corner.

"Help me with that." He gestured toward the box.

Together, the brothers lifted the crate, wincing at every creak of the ancient wood. They positioned it below the window, and Paul climbed up first, balancing precariously on the weathered slats. The crate wobbled under his weight, threatening to collapse.

"Steady now." Dan braced the box with his hands.

Paul reached up, his fingers brushing against the window frame. He found a metal latch and tried to turn it. Years of disuse had seized it in place. He applied more pressure. "No dice. It's rusted solid."

"How about breaking out the rest of the glass?"

Paul shook his head. "Too noisy. And with the opening so narrow, we could cut ourselves to ribbons crawling through." He hopped onto the floor.

Dan tilted his head toward the basement stairs leading to the hall. "Only one way out, then."

Paul nodded grimly. The brothers walked to the bottom of the stairs.

"We need to be absolutely silent." Dan's mouth was so close to Paul's ear that his breath stirred his brother's hair. "There hasn't been a sound from them up there for a while, but they still could be upstairs. One noise and we could be done for."

"Those stairs look ancient," Paul said. "They'll sing like canaries if we just walk up to them."

"They do. I've been on them once already," Dan said. "See the edges? Along the wall. The wood is not as worn there."

"Less traffic, less wear. Is that what you're saying?" Paul peered at the treads.

"Yeah. If we go in single file, right on the edge where the steps meet the wall, we avoid the worst creaks." Dan pointed to the narrow strip of wood that ran alongside the wall. "The nails will be more secure there, too, where the tread connects to the support."

Paul looked skeptical. "You're positive about that?"

"No," Dan shrugged.

"You're so reassuring."

"It worked for me the last time, but I was alone," Dan said. "I'll go first. Follow exactly where I step and go slowly. Very slowly. If anything starts to creak, freeze until it settles."

Paul reached out and squeezed his brother's shoulder. "Let's go."

Dan took a deep breath and placed one foot on the bottom stair, pressing his weight against the wall, balancing on the outermost edge of the tread. The aged wood accepted his weight without protest. He brought his other foot up to join the first, moving with the deliberate precision of a tightrope walker. When both feet were secure, he looked back at Paul and waved him along.

The second step proved more of a challenge. As Dan shifted his body forward, a slight groan came from the tread. He froze instantly, his muscles tensing, breath caught in his throat. After ten agonizing seconds, Dan resumed his glacial pace, easing onto the next with tremendous care. Paul followed, mimicking Dan's movements, placing each foot precisely where his brother had stepped. The brothers continued up the stairs with the concentration of two mountaineers scaling a treacherous peak.

Dan finally reached the top of the stairs, Paul joining him moments later, their shoulders brushing in the confined space. They stood motionless, ears straining for any sound from the other side.

Leaning forward, Dan pressed his ear against the wooden door. The grain was rough against his skin, tiny splinters threatening to embed themselves in his cheek. He closed his eyes, focusing all his attention on listening.

Had the gang left already? Or were they returning to perform their grisly task? Had they changed their minds about drowning the brothers?

The last thought sent a surge of hope through Dan, but he quashed it. He doubted the Professor would do that, so he continued listening. Dan pulled back and met Paul's questioning gaze. He gave a small shrug, then shook his head.

Paul nodded and gestured toward the door, a silent question in his eyes: Should they risk it?

Dan hesitated. If the gang was still inside, opening the door would reveal their escape. But remaining in the basement was just as dangerous. They'd be trapped when someone eventually came to check on them or, worse, to make good on the Professor's plan.

Decision made, Dan reached for the doorknob. The metal was cool beneath his fingers as he gripped it firmly. He tested it first, applying the gentlest pressure, feeling for resistance. The knob turned easily in his hand. He pulled the door open a crack and peeked out.

The small hallway was empty. Dan craned his neck, getting a view of the office. The printing press was gone.

"I think they've left, or at least are out by the truck," Dan said to Paul in a soft voice. "Let's get out of here while we have a chance."

"No need to say that again, my dear brother," Paul replied. "I don't like this hotel."

The pair headed for the exterior door. Dan was about to open it when he heard voices. They froze, Dan's hand hovering over the doorknob.

"Is the equipment loaded?" The Professor's clipped, precise tones cut through the air. He sounded as if he were standing outside by the basement doors.

"Yes, sir," came Rocky's response. "The press, the plates, the paper, and the finished product. It's all in the truck."

"Did you wipe everything down?" the Professor asked.

"Two times," Tommy answered. "Not a print left in the place."

"Good," the Professor said. "This location has served its purpose. Now we need to tie up those loose ends."

Dan and Paul exchanged glances. The twins were the loose ends. And with the gang just outside, the brothers couldn't make a run for it.

"Vic, Tommy," the Professor continued. "Go down to the boiler room and bring up our young friends. And remember what I said — not a single mark on them. Nothing that would contradict the drowning story. No bruises, no cuts, nothing. Is that understood?"

"Yes, Professor," Vic said.

"We got it," Tommy added.

"Good. We'll wait here while you get them." The Professor said. "No, not through that door inside. Enter through these out here.

It is more direct. And do not let them touch anything. We don't want any fingerprints at all."

"Got it," Vic said. "Tommy, open the doors. No, not like that. Use your handkerchief."

There was rattling and creaking as the bulkhead doors opened.

"Be right back," Vic said. His and Tommy's footsteps faded down the stairs.

Chapter Eleven

After a few minutes, the voices of Vic and Tommy erupted from the basement: "They're gone!" Their footsteps thundered on the stairs as they ran back outside to the Professor.

"They've escaped!" Vic said, sounding like he was catching his breath.

"Gone! Mousey, you told me when you tied them up, they would stay tied up!" Rocky shouted. Mousey's pained yelp followed a loud slap. "I oughta—"

"Rocky, stop that," the Professor commanded. "That is of no help to us right now. Vic, did you and Tommy check the entire basement?"

"No, Professor. We thought it better to —" Tommy said.

"Enough," the Professor interrupted. "We need to think logically." There was a brief pause. "When we were packing and relocating the printing press, the basement exterior doors were secured. Correct?"

"Right. Me and Tommy locked them after we packed up the dough," Vic answered.

"Rocky and I were still on the first floor at the time. Thus, the only exit route available to them would have been the inside stairs from the basement," the Professor said. "That would have required them to pass by the office, and we would have observed them."

"Yeah, we would have," Rocky said. "We didn't budge the whole time."

"Mousey, did you see them anywhere on the way to the truck? Any signs they passed by?" the Professor asked.

"No," Mousey replied.

"Vic and Tommy, you were returning to the mill when we met you out here. Did you see anything?" the Professor asked.

"Nothing," Vic said.

"We didn't see them exit the building. Every window is either boarded up or has shutters. All are locked except for the three, this one and two upstairs. That leaves the logical assumption they're still inside," the Professor said.

"Alright, Vic and Tommy, you two take the —" Rocky started.

The Professor cut him off. "No, Rocky. That will never do. We will perform this search in an organized manner. Not like fowls with their heads removed."

A "huh?" came from Tommy.

The Professor ignored him. "Vic, are you armed?"

"Yeah."

"I'm afraid the drowning scenario may no longer be possible, but I hope we can still use it. Vic, you remain outside and cover this area. If they try to force a window on the other side, you'll hear it and can reach the location quickly. You are to keep those two boys from leaving the mill. I prefer them alive, but in all cases, stop them. By any means necessary," the Professor said.

"Right," Vic responded. "I got it."

"Rocky, you, Mousey, Tommy and I will start in the basement. There are many... what is the term? 'Nooks and crannies.' Is that correct?" the Professor asked.

"Yeah, that's it," Rocky said.

"Bon. There are many nooks and crannies that those two could use to hide in the cellar," the Professor said. "After we complete searching below, we will do the first floor, and so on. Everything is to be done in a methodical and organized manner. Is that understood?"

The entire gang answered "right" at once.

"Vic, secure these doors after we go down," the Professor said crisply.

"Okay."

Footsteps echoed as they descended the stairs to the basement, followed by the closing of the outside doors and the rasp of the latch locking. Dan pulled Paul through the door into the hall and closed it.

The Professor said something downstairs that Dan couldn't understand — more directions, he guessed — and the cellar grew silent. They had already started their search. Time was slipping away.

Dan scanned his surroundings, searching for any options. Escaping through the window in the office would land them smack in front of Vic. The door to the open back of the mill — where the saw blade was — was barred. It was impossible for Dan and Paul to go back downstairs. The tiny room where Dan was first held captive lacked any windows. That left a single way out: the door to the right of the basement one.

Dan jerked his head toward it, tugging Paul in that direction. Old hinges protested with a soft creak as Dan eased the door open, praying the sound wouldn't carry to the basement. The doorway revealed a set of steps.

The staircase was narrow and steep, constructed of weathered wooden planks that were worn by years of boots before being abandoned. Dim light filtered through the small, dust-covered windows at the top landing, casting long shadows down the steps.

The first step creaked under Dan, freezing both boys in place. They held their breath, listening for any reaction from below. After several agonizing seconds of silence, Dan continued upward, testing each stair before committing his full weight. Paul closed the door behind him and followed.

Dan thought about what they might uncover on the upper level. The second floor might offer an escape route. Perhaps they could discover a window that opened onto a part of the roof. They could climb out and possibly find a way down to the ground. Maybe one window on the side away from where Vic was guarding would open quietly.

Or it could be another dead end, a more effective trap than what they were in.

The sounds from the basement grew distant — the Professor's gang must be checking every inch of the space, just as ordered. The brothers had minutes at most before the search party would move to the first floor.

Halfway up the stairs, Paul stumbled, catching himself against the wall with a thud that seemed to echo through the empty building. Both boys froze again.

"What was that?" Tommy's voice carried faintly from the cellar.

"Just the old structure settling," the Professor replied. "Continue searching."

Dan released a quiet breath and locked eyes with Paul, their mutual relief unspoken. They turned their attention back to the staircase, a few steps creaking underfoot as they climbed with caution. The landing was close. Beyond the head of the stairs lay the unknown of the second floor — either their way out or a complete dead end in this life-and-death game of hide-and-seek.

They reached the landing, and some floorboards greeted them with creaks beneath their feet, a chorus of age and wear. The air on the upper story hung thick and still, a mix of humidity and decay, with the musty aroma of aged timber and mildew swirling around it.

Dan held a finger to his lips, though the warning was unnecessary. Before them stretched a narrow corridor with weathered wainscoting running along the walls. Four doors — two on each side — lined up, guarding whatever secrets and escape routes this floor contained. All were closed, their once-white paint now yellowed and peeling, revealing darker wood underneath like old scars.

"We don't have much time," Dan's voice was barely audible.

Dan gently nudged open the first door on his right, just enough to peek into the room. It must have been an office once. At the center stood a large oak desk, its surface spotless, contrasting with the thick dust coating the rest of the room. Dan figured it had been cleaned, as the Professor had instructed. There was one window across from the door, its shutter drawn. Dan didn't need to move any closer to see the padlock securely fastening it from the inside.

"Nothing," Dan said in a soft voice, easing the door closed.

The floorboards, worn and creaky, thankfully remained silent beneath their cautious footsteps as they tiptoed to the next room. Dan placed his hand on the knob and felt a slight resistance. Warped, perhaps. He leaned his shoulder into it, and with a gentle push, it at last swung open. The room was bare, its walls unadorned, and the floor empty. Just like the previous one, the window shutter was firmly latched, only allowing a glint of sunlight around the edges.

The brothers moved swiftly as they crossed the hallway to reach a door on the other side. Inside the room, a wooden table surrounded by four mismatched chairs stood, their surfaces wiped down, out of place with the dusty, cluttered surroundings. The air carried a lingering aroma of pork and beans. This must have been the spot where the gang cooked and ate their meals.

The shutter in this room was ajar. Dan and Paul crept toward it and peered through the small gap. Below, Vic leaned against the mill's door, wisps of smoke curling from the cigarette held between his fingers, as casual as if waiting for a bus. It was clear they couldn't make their escape that way. Not only did a dangerous two-story drop await them, but Vic's eyes would catch them the moment they tried.

From below came the distinct sound of footsteps on the basement stairs. The search party must be moving up to the first floor.

The brothers stepped into the last room, and Dan had to admit to himself, their last hope. It held two makeshift bunk beds, each cobbled together with rough wood. The towering bedposts stretched upward, almost grazing the ceiling, and were dotted with a haphazard array of hooks and nails, most likely used to hang clothes, although only some rope hung from one post now. The mattresses sagged in the middle, and their surfaces were riddled with lumps. The gang ate next door and slept here.

The twins turned toward the shutter. That window presented the same problems as the other one: a long, direct drop in front of Vic. No way out of here, either.

The Professor's voice came from downstairs. "Tommy, stand by the outside door. Mousey, stay by the basement door. Rocky and I will check the office. It won't take long."

"We're trapped," Paul whispered. "If you've got any bright ideas, my dear brother, now's the time to spread them around... like manure."

Dan ran his fingers through his hair, mind racing. The scratchy sound of footsteps moving across the floor below confirmed their time was almost up. His eyes darted around the room, searching for anything that could be used. "Look." He pointed to a narrow door in the corner.

Paul put his lips next to Dan's ear. "A closet?"

Dan gave a shrug and approached the door. He cracked it open just enough to reveal a small space just large enough for a ladder attached to one wall, leading to a trapdoor in the ceiling. Paul squeezed in behind his brother.

"Attic?" Paul asked.

Dan nodded.

"So we go up?"

Dan paused to think, then shook his head. "That would really box us in. Let's make them *think* we've gone up there." He pushed Paul toward the bunk beds. "Duck under the bottom bunk, slide all the way back to the wall. Like when we were kids, playing hide 'n seek with Dad. Remember?"

Paul nodded and wedged himself into the tight space beneath the bunk, pushing up against the wall, disappearing from view. Scrambling up the ladder, Dan flung the trapdoor open with a loud bang.

"Professor!" Mousey's excited voice carried clearly through the old building. "Professor! I heard something upstairs — like a door or something opening!"

A moment of silence followed, broken only by the distant sound of Vic coughing outside.

"Are you certain?" The Professor was calm, but his tone betrayed an underlying tension.

"So did I! I heard it, too!" Tommy added.

"Yes, sir! Sounded like it came from up above — maybe one of the doors upstairs?" Mousey went on.

Dan's heart was pounding in his chest as he returned to the floor and crawled under the other bunk, shoving his body as far back as possible. This was their only chance. If the gang didn't buy the trick, neither twin would have a way out. He focused on calming his breath.

"Interesting." The Professor took on that cold, clinical tone Dan had come to dread. "Very interesting indeed. It appears our young friends are more resourceful than we anticipated. But they made a terrible choice. There is no way out of that floor. They are trapped like rats."

Heavy footfalls crossed the first floor, followed by the creak of the staircase. The Professor grew louder as he issued commands. "Everyone upstairs. Now. Remember, gentlemen, I want them alive — if possible. I would still desire their demise to appear accidental."

The stairs snapped and popped under multiple sets of feet. Dan pressed himself further against the wall, almost as if trying to become part of the wood itself. The footsteps reached the landing.

From his hiding place, Dan only saw a sliver of the room — the lower half of a heavy oak office chair across from him, the worn planks, and the bottom of the door. The cramped space was suffocating, the air thick with decades of accumulated dust and the musty scent of neglect. A spider scurried past Dan's face, disappearing into the shadows behind him.

"Check each room one at a time," the Professor ordered, his voice now alarmingly close. "They are clever, I must admit, but they are still just boys."

The door to the first room opened with a creak, followed by sounds of movement and cursing from Rocky. "Nothin' here, Professor."

The second door swung open and then closed, then the third. Dan found it hard to breathe as the footsteps neared the room where they were hiding. The door creaked, swung wide, and a pair of worn shoes stepped inside. From his place under the bunk, Dan saw Tommy's feet come into view as he carefully entered the room.

Tommy halted. "Professor!" He spoke in a harsh whisper, his voice rising with excitement. "Professor, come look at this!"

The floorboards outside groaned as heavier footfalls approached. Polished black shoes appeared in the doorway.

"What is it, Tommy?" The Professor's voice was taut with anticipation.

Tommy's scuffed shoes shifted toward the corner. "That door — it's open! I know I closed it!" He moved to the doorway. "And look up — the trapdoor to the attic is open too! I bet those guys went up there."

"Hmm." The Professor turned as he assessed the situation. "Yes, I believe you're right. That explains the noise Mousey heard. Very good, Tommy."

More feet entered the room — Rocky's leather boots and Mousey's smaller, cheaper sneakers.

"We got 'em now," Rocky said, a cruel eagerness in his voice. "They thought they were smart... maybe crawl out on the roof and climb down to the ground that way. But that ladder is the only way out of the attic. They ain't goin' nowhere."

"Indeed," the Professor said.

"There's lots of stuff up there, Professor. Boxes and things," said Rocky. "A lot of places to hide."

"And cornered rodents do fight, and even may become dangerous," the Professor said. "Nevertheless, we continue with my plan. We will all go up and sweep the area as a team. Walk the length of the attic, side by side. Mousey, you remain down here, just in case."

"Three of us versus two of them in a closed space," Tommy said with a harsh chuckle. "They're cooked."

"Tommy, you go first. Then myself, and Rocky last," the Professor directed. "Be careful. Those boys are most likely desperate, and they could resort to desperate measures. They could use anything as a weapon."

Tommy grabbed the rungs of the wooden ladder, testing them before he began to climb. "Seems sturdy enough," he said, climbing toward the open trapdoor. The wood creaked as he did, each sound magnified in the tense silence.

The Professor started up next, his movements precise and methodical, as if even in pursuit, he maintained his dignity. Rocky brought up the rear, his bulk almost completely filling the small closet and causing the ladder to complain under his weight.

Dan held his breath as he listened to the muffled thuds of their footsteps disappear into the attic. The sounds became more distant as they moved along the floor above, accompanied by the occasional curse as someone tripped over an unseen obstacle in the shadows.

"Spread out," the Professor's voice, muted by the ceiling, gave the command. "Check behind every box, inside every trunk. Stay in a row, alongside me. We'll move to the far end. Flush them out."

The creaking footsteps crept across the attic floorboards. A fine layer of dust drifted down through the narrow cracks in the ceiling, creating a shimmering veil in the light as the men searched.

"What a pile of junk up here," Rocky complained, his voice followed by the sound of something heavy being shoved aside. "They should'va taken this stuff when the place shut down."

"Be thorough. Check everywhere," the Professor said. "They might be hiding anywhere."

Dan mouthed the numbers as he counted to twenty, his pulse quickening with each silent tick. He listened to the muffled sounds of the four gang members rummaging through dusty boxes and old trunks in the attic. When Dan was sure they had moved away from the trapdoor, he slid out from under the sagging wooden bunk, like an animal emerging from its den. He cast a quick glance into Paul's hiding place and urgently gestured for his brother to follow him.

Mousey stood in the doorway to the closet, peering up the ladder, his back to the room.

The search continued from above. "Check that eave," the Professor said. "Move those crates."

A scraping sound came from the floor over the twins' heads —some trunk being moved aside, probably — causing a fresh cascade of dust to spill through the ceiling cracks like a gritty waterfall. Dan decided it was time to give Mousey a closer look.

He darted towards the attic door and shoved Mousey inside. Closing the door, Dan leaned against it and pointed at the solid oak office chair, then signaled toward the door with a swift wave of his hand. Paul caught the silent command immediately. He hurried to the chair, picked it up and carried it to his brother.

Paul wedged the back of the chair under the doorknob. Together, the brothers kicked the chair's rear legs, jamming it tightly against the handle. Mousey began yelling and pounding on the door.

Then, from above, came the Professor's cold, precise tone. "What is going on?"

"They're down here!" Mousey's panicked voice pierced through the door.

"What!" Tommy yelled. "What did you say?"

"I said they're down here!" Mousey repeated.

The realization seemed to hit the gang at once, setting off a frantic rush. Boots and shoes pounded along the creaky attic floor. The ancient wooden beams protested with loud creaks and groans from the sudden shift of weight of the four men racing for the trapdoor.

"Come on!" Dan grabbed Paul's arm, pulling him in the direction of the hallway. "We've got to get out of here before Vic hears them, or they break through!"

Paul grinned. "Too bad. I was beginning to enjoy the show." The brothers darted toward the corridor. "Wait!" Paul snagged the rope hanging on the post.

"They were hiding in the room the whole time!" Tommy yelled, his voice a mixture of rage and disbelief. "They tricked us! Made us think they went upstairs! Nobody makes a fool of me! When I get my hands on those guys, they're gonna wish they were never born."

"Shut up and get outta my way, punk!" Rocky boomed, followed by the sound of someone being shoved aside. "I said move, Tommy, you idiot!"

"Gentlemen, please!" The Professor's voice cut through the commotion, still maintaining its eerie composure despite what was happening. "Order is essential, even in haste."

"Mousey, get up here! There isn't enough room for both of us down there! Hurry! Get outta my way, I said!" Rocky demanded.

Mousey's footsteps scrambled to the attic. Rocky landed on the ladder with enough force to make Dan wonder if it might collapse because of his size, creaking dangerously as Rocky descended. A sharp crack suggested one rung had given way under his bulk, followed by Rocky's curse.

In the hallway, Paul closed the door. He tied one end of the rope around the knob.

"I catch!" Dan said. He took the other end of the rope, stretched it tight and knotted it to the knob of the shut door across the hall.

"It's jammed!" Rocky's muffled voice came through the door, accompanied by the violent sound of the doorknob rattling.

"They've blocked it, the little—" He hammered on the door. "Vic! Vic! Get up here!"

The sounds of chaos from the attic grew louder. Rocky pounded on the door, yelling Vic's name.

Grinning, the twins rushed down the stairs. About halfway, the door at the bottom swung open to reveal Vic. His eyes first widened in surprise, then narrowed with a menacing look. For a moment, it was hard to tell who was more surprised.

Chapter Twelve

After a shocked moment, Vic reached into his right coat pocket. The butt of his gun appeared in his hand as he started to pull it out.

"Going somewhere, boys?" he asked.

Paul whispered, barely moving his lips. "Do what I do, but go the other way."

Dan gave an almost imperceptible nod, his body tensing for action. The air between all three thickened, taut and crackling with electricity.

Paul took a deep breath, then suddenly flung himself forward, not at Vic, but at the wall of the stairwell. He pushed off it like a swimmer at the turn, launching his body in a diagonal path that sent him crashing into the opposite side. Dan copied the movement, but in the other direction.

The confined space amplified the chaos. Paul and Dan's bodies became twin pinballs ricocheting in the narrow stairwell.

The brothers' unexpected moves left Vic startled and confused. He waved the gun erratically, his narrowed eyes darting between the two, trying to guess who was coming at him next, or which one was his target.

Paul made a final push off the wall with explosive force and slammed into Vic with the might of a freight train. The impact drove all the air from Vic's lungs as the pair tumbled to the floor at the bottom of the stairs. Paul landed on top of Vic, one knee crashing hard into his side. The revolver flew from Vic's hand, skidding across the worn wooden floorboards.

The two grappled and tussled, rolling over the rough planks, grunting as they traded punches. Paul swung a right hook that connected with a solid thud against Vic's jaw, sending a jolt up his arm. Vic quickly retaliated, sending his fist into Paul's lip. Their bodies twisted in a brutal, messy tangle, the battle more animal-like than skilled.

Dan burst into the melee as though breaking up a schoolyard brawl. He grabbed Vic under his arms. With a forceful yank, Dan heaved Vic to his feet. Paul, breathing heavily, scrambled upright, his fists clenched, ready to deliver another punch.

Vic twisted sharply in Dan's hold, his elbow shooting back and driving hard into Dan's stomach. Dan gasped at the blow. He staggered backward, his foot catching on the cold metal of a gun lying on the floor. Dan reached down and snatched up the weapon, his fingers curling around the grip. He swung around, ready to use it to halt the fight.

At the same time, Paul charged. Vic moved swiftly to the side, his movements smooth and fluid like a jungle cat. Vic seized Paul's arm with a firm grasp, using the teen's own speed to hurl him forward.

Paul stumbled, his feet scrambling to find balance, before he crashed into Dan. The collision wrenched the revolver out of Dan's hand and sent it spinning through the air, landing with a sharp metallic clatter near the stairs. Vic darted to retrieve it.

Not a word passed between the brothers; their communication was silent. They launched themselves at Vic as one. Dan lunged low, wrapping his arms around Vic's knees, while Paul tackled Vic's waist. Vic's eyes widened as their coordinated assault took him by surprise.

Vic let out a guttural curse as the double jolt hit, driving him sideways. He staggered, his arms flailing wildly in a futile attempt to regain his balance. With a final, bone-jarring crash, the trio smashed into an old wooden crate next to the basement door. The box splintered under their combined weight, sending up a cloud of dust and jagged shards of wood. Vic lay sprawled among the debris of shattered wood, knocked cold in the fall.

Paul rolled away, panting. Dan sat back and wiped dirt from his cheek. They exchanged glances and smiled like kids who had executed the perfect April Fool's joke.

"I guess it's true twins can read each other's minds," Dan said as he knelt by Vic.

"Didn't you know that?" Paul also got on one knee by the unconscious gang member. He picked up the snub-nosed revolver off the floor and handed it to Dan. "Here. Merry Christmas."

Dan took the gun. "Golly, gee, thanks, mister! Just what I always wanted! A lethal weapon!"

"Don't play with it indoors." Paul removed Vic's belt and used it to tie Vic's hands behind his back. From the floor above, the banging and thumping on the attic door continued, growing louder with each second.

Dan pointed towards a chair in the office and shut the stairway door. Paul understood Dan's plan, dashed into the office, and seized the chair. Together, they jammed it beneath the doorknob, like they did with the one upstairs.

"Now, put Vic in here." Dan opened the door to the room where he had been held captive. Paul dragged the unconscious gang member inside. When he came back out, Dan closed the door and slid the bolt.

"Time to take a powder." Paul jerked his head toward the noise. "They'll figure out Vic isn't coming and start to break out soon."

The two ran out of the mill and stopped.

"When's the next streetcar?" Paul asked.

"I don't have a timetable with me," Dan said. "We'll have to walk."

"Yeah, but which way? Where do we go?" Paul glanced around. "We're surrounded by the swamp, and they've sunk the canoe."

"There's a way out of here somewhere nearby," Dan said. "They didn't lug a printing press all the way to some point by a distant highway. They must have a truck. I mean, they said they did."

Paul lifted his hands in a helpless gesture. "So where is it? Is it invisible?"

"No, but has to be close, so there's got to be some kind of way to reach it," Dan said. "Let's find out."

Dan and Paul sprinted down the hard-packed dirt next to the old mill. They reached the far corner of the building and scanned the area. The massive, rusted saw blade loomed silently, still fixed in its position inside the structure's open end. The narrow, muddy canal snaked its way from the swamp directly to the open maw, the water's murky surface catching and reflecting the sun's rays in a dance of shimmering patterns.

"That's probably how they got the cut trees from the swamp to the saw. Floated them in." Dan pointed to the water. "There's the way in, so there also must have been a way they got the sawed planks out of here. A road or a cart road or something." He scanned the surroundings again, hoping to discover something suggesting a path.

Dan slapped the back of his hand against Paul's shoulder and jerked his head toward the other end of the building. They dashed back.

Inside, the noise of Rocky's pounding on the wooden door echoed throughout the mill. The door seemed to be remaining strong, keeping the gang confined in the attic. The real question was, how much longer would the old wood hold?

"He's going to bust down that door sooner or later," Dan said in a worried voice.

"Here, Dan!" Paul stopped and waved at the ground. "Look! Check out the ground! There are old-fashioned wagon ruts running off that way! Even though this dirt is hard as cement, there are other tracks, like something being dragged along in the same direction. Or wheels, like a dolly carrying something heavy." He shielded his eyes from the sun with one hand and pointed with the other. "That must be it! Follow those ruts! The road is off that way."

"Let's go. It should lead to the truck the gang are using. When we find it, we'll take it." Dan clapped one hand on Paul's shoulder.

"My dear brother, I'm shocked! Are you suggesting we boost a vehicle?" Paul said in mock horror.

Dan leaned toward Paul. "We'll just call it 'borrowing without asking permission of the owner' in case anybody asks. Come on, let's make tracks before Rocky smashes down that door."

The brothers took off running, their feet thudding on the hardened dirt. Dense forest bordered their path on either side, like a massing army ready to invade the worn road. Occasionally, clusters of shrubs crept onto the trail, their leaves whispering in the breeze. One bush jutted out farther than the others, as if testing boundaries. A lone sapling staked out a place in the center of the path, its slender branches reaching toward the sky.

Soon the old road became little more than a suggestion, squeezing down to a narrow trail where nature was winning its slow, relentless battle to take back the land from the outsider humans. Thick roots snaked along what once might have been smooth ground, creating natural hurdles that threatened to trip them with each stride. Overhead, branches from opposing trees reached across to touch, forming a cathedral-like canopy.

"Watch your step," Paul called over his shoulder, jumping over a fallen log that had been consumed by emerald moss. "This place is a regular obstacle course."

Dan followed, his breath coming in controlled bursts. "No wonder they didn't drive their truck up to the mill. You'd need a machete to get through some of this."

"And the reason Rocky complained about moving everything. It must have been a pain in the neck to haul stuff through here," Paul said.

As they ran, the forest pressed in closer with each passing minute as if an impatient mob, the underbrush growing denser on either side. The brothers came to an abrupt halt as the path ahead vanished beneath a tangle of vegetation.

What was a narrow trail now appeared completely stopped by a wall of green. Trees, tall grasses, and thick bushes had overgrown this section of the old road.

"Well, this is just spiffy," Paul muttered, placing his fists on his hips as he surveyed the obstacle. "Road's gone. Looks like we hit a dead end. There has to be another way to the mill. We must have missed it."

"There wasn't any other I saw. No, they had to go this way, unless they sprouted wings and flew," Dan said. "You've got to hand it to the Professor, though. Most people wouldn't think anybody would be crazy enough to move equipment through all this to the old mill. The gang made the place secure and secret."

"Until we messed it up," Paul added.

"That's us," Dan said. "Always upsetting the apple cart."

Dan stepped forward. He reached out and pressed down hard on one of the bushes blocking their path. The plant bent easily under his hand, but the moment he released it, the branches sprang back to their original position with surprising force.

"These aren't old growth," Dan observed, rubbing his thumb and forefinger together to feel the residue from the fresh, green stem. "This stuff's new. Maybe a few years at most."

"That's fascinating, Daniel Boone, but so what?" Paul jerked his head toward the mill. "We're going to have company pretty soon. It won't take Rocky long to break down that door once he realizes Vic isn't coming, and he sets his little pea brain to the job."

"Wait, I've got an idea. Look, the gang must have gone this way. The path they used could continue around on one side or the other of this foliage. Let's split up. You take the left," Dan gestured at the greenery in front of them, "I'll take the right. Stay within earshot."

"What are we looking for?" Paul asked, already moving in the direction of his assigned side. "A sign saying 'this way to the truck'?"

"No, dope. Check for clues that suggest somebody passed through here," Dan explained. "Footprints, broken twigs, that type of thing."

Paul nodded in understanding. "Like an unmaintained trail they used. The path still exists, but it's not obvious."

"You got it, my dear brother." Dan began to examine the ground near the edge of the roadway. "Look for patterns, disturbances, anything. Nature is random, but people leave signs."

"Especially if they're dragging heavy equipment," Paul added. "They didn't float parts of a printing press through the air like a magician doing a levitation trick. They'd have to leave some kind of mark."

The brothers separated, each moving slowly along their re-spective side of the overgrown road. The brush on Paul's side was thick, forcing him to push through layers of tangled vegeta-tion. Leaves scraped against his face, and the occasional branch clutched at him.

He moved forward, breaking through the bushes sooner than he had expected. About two feet in width of the old road was still visible, with growth on either side. His eyes scanned the ground for any hints that the gang had passed through. If they did, some traces had to be left.

No signs turned up that Paul could see, and he was beginning to suspect he was heading the wrong way. This route couldn't possibly be the one the gang used to reach their truck. They must have gone in the other direction, the one Dan was searching.

He was about to give up when something glinted among the fallen leaves and twigs — a flash of reflected light that didn't be-long in nature. Dan crouched down, pushing aside the branches of a small bush.

His fingers closed around the smooth surface of a glass bottle. He lifted it up, turning it in his hands. It was an empty soda bottle, the label still bright and clean. No moss or algae had begun to grow on it; the cap was missing, but the rim was still sticky with dried residue.

"This hasn't been here long," he muttered to himself. He remembered Tommy telling Vic about his soda. It could be his.

This could be evidence that the gang members used this route he needed. Paul stood, dropping the bottle and brushing off his hands. He continued his search with renewed energy, inspecting the ground ahead.

Now that he hoped he was on the right track, the signs became more obvious to him — a patch of moss recently disturbed, broken twigs with the exposed wood still pale and fresh, a depression in the soft earth that could only be a footprint.

Paul traced these faint clues, taking the path where the old road would have existed, but had not been completely swallowed by the forest. As the vegetation started to thin out, Paul came across a definite trail winding through the trees. It looked like it had been used not too long ago — the underbrush was crushed in spots, and some branches had been broken off by somebody pushing through. Paul went on.

As he advanced, the thick brush receded all at once, as if deciding to abandon the path, leaving it bare and unclaimed. Increasing his speed, Paul jogged over the packed dirt as it grew into a recognizable road again. Rounding a curve, he arrived at a sunlit clearing, which was a broad section of the road lined by the swamp on two sides.

A new navy blue Buick Roadmaster was parked in this area, its chrome vertical grille shining in the sunlight like a grinning shark. Next to the car, a rugged Ford half-ton truck stood, reminding Paul of an old military vehicle. A faded, olive green canvas canopy tightly stretched over a robust wire frame covered the bed.

Paul punched the air in victory. "Our chariots await!"

He'd found a way to escape this place. Now to go back and get Dan.

***

Dan shoved aside branches, searching the forest floor for any indication of human passage. He growled in irritation as the branch he pushed away bounced back and slapped him in the face, leaving a thin scratch across his cheek. His frustration grew with each step, every crunch of dried leaves underfoot mirroring his mounting impatience. Then he stepped into what appeared to be a meadow.

"Finally," he muttered.

In front of him lay an open space. On the other side, he could make out a relatively clear, wide break in the trees. It looked to be exactly what he was searching for — the continuation of the road. The flat area between him and the tree gap was strewn with dead branches and other vegetation.

The ground was damp, with small reeds and patches of vivid green moss growing rimming the edge. Off to one side, he saw the swamp right next to the area, so Dan thought the water was flowing over the road as well, hiding it from view.

This must be the right track, he thought. The truck had to be nearby, maybe on the other side of this open space, just beyond those trees. He began to jog, eager to cross the clearing. His shoes squelched in the water with every step.

About halfway across, something seemed wrong to him. The ground beneath his feet didn't feel firm. Instead, it gave way a little, wiggled. Dan faltered mid-stride, his momentum carrying him forward even as alarm bells rang in his head. After another few steps, he sank ankle-deep into what he'd thought was solid earth.

"What the —" Dan flapped his arms, trying to regain his balance. The gun flew from his hand, splashed into the water and disappeared from sight. But the more Dan tried to free his feet, the lower he went. Then it registered in his brain what was going on...

Quicksand. He was caught in a quicksand pit.

He'd just spent what seemed like hours freeing himself and Paul to escape the gang, and now this. It just wasn't fair.

The stuff seeped over the tops of his sneakers and oozed between his toes. The sludge crept over his ankles and calves with the weight of a python made of wet cement.

He tried to wrench his leg free, only to realize his error. With every movement, he sank deeper, the quicksand's tug strengthening. It held to his bare skin, a cruel combination of slickness and grit, coiling around his thighs with an unyielding force, pulling him down with merciless tenacity.

By the time the stuff reached his waist, the pressure was heavy, as if a ton of mud was determined to snap him like a twig. His swimsuit was plastered to his waist. The sand clung relentlessly, an abrasive, cold and dense muck, biting into his flesh with every futile attempt to pull free.

His upper body remained above the surface, but teetered on the brink of being swallowed whole. The damp air reeked of earth and decay, a pungent mix of rot and stagnant water. Dan froze, gasping for breath. Each slight movement only made the quicksand's grip more vicious, tightening like a vice.

"Paul!" he shouted, fear rising in his throat. "Paul! Help!"

Dan tried a last chance lunge toward the edge, but the violent motion only caused him sink more. Within seconds, he was stomach-deep in the mire, the quicksand pulling him deeper. He grabbed in desperation at a nearby reed, but it came loose in his hand, roots and all.

"PAUL!" The shout tore from his lungs as the cold, wet gunk reached the bottom of his rib cage. The gun taken from Vic was now somewhere beneath him, lost in the murky depths. He couldn't use it to signal his brother.

Dan forced himself to stop thrashing, remembering something he'd once read about quicksand — that panic was the real killer. Fighting against every instinct, he tried to remain still, but he continued to sink.

The mud crawled up to just below his chest, thick and suffocating. The edge of the clearing, which had appeared so close moments ago, now looked impossibly distant. The weight of the sand pressed on him, making each breath a struggle.

All those jungle movies he'd watched over the years flooded into his mind, images of people sucked into the mire and disappearing.

How long would it take before his head would be under the surface?

Chapter Thirteen

Paul headed back toward where he and Dan had separated. Then, a thought stopped him.

Keys.

He hadn't considered them. He looked over his shoulder at the parked truck and car. Perhaps he should go back to check if the keys were still in the ignition. Without them, the vehicles would be of no use.

Paul was about to retrace his steps when a distant voice reached his ears, causing him to freeze. He tilted his head, straining to catch the sound again, and there it came again — a shout that unmistakably carried his name.

It was his brother calling, tinged with urgency and fear, as if he needed help. Paul reacted immediately, charging through the dense underbrush, the sharp branches clawing at his arms and legs as he hurried back to the spot where he and Dan had split up.

The area was empty. Paul scanned the ground, searching for the faint trail his twin had left behind. A series of scuffed leaves and bent stems pointed the way, and he set off in that direction.

Paul pressed on, weaving his way through the thick bushes. At last, he burst out of the forest and found himself at the edge of an open area bathed in sunlight. What he saw there stunned him.

Dan was in the center of a clearing, buried up to his chest in dark, loose soil. His face was a mixture of fear and exhaustion, beads of sweat glistening on his forehead. Paul moved toward his brother. The dirt under his feet grew spongy. It was a weird sensation, and he froze mid-step.

"Paul, stop! Quicksand!" Dan yelled. His arms were still free, and he waved his twin back. "No farther! Go back!"

Paul stumbled backward. After a second, he cautiously tested the firmness of the ground with one foot. The dirt was springy, almost as if the earth was making up its mind to hold steady under his weight or not. Inch by inch, he edged closer to the quagmire until he felt it was safe.

Kneeling down, he put one arm out as far as he could toward his brother. Dan reached back, his fingers clawing at the air. Their fingertips brushed the space between them — but not close enough. With an angry growl, Paul pushed himself back up. He stood and began to pace. Time to figure out Plan B.

"I'll find something," Paul said to Dan. His eyes scanned the surroundings. They fixed on a fallen tree branch nearby. It looked strong and appeared long enough to reach.

Paul dove for the branch, the rough bark pressing into his hand as he grabbed it. He wrapped his other arm around the tree trunk, held a wooden lifeline toward Dan. "Grab it!" He knew it was a useless instruction, and a completely stupid one at that.

Dan clawed at the air, grimaces etching hard lines on his face. Paul strained as he tried to eke out an extra inch or two to his reach, attempting to close the final gap between the branch and his brother's hand. Dan made a desperate clutch for the limb, fingers grazing it. Paul forced himself to stretch even more, the ground threatening to give way underneath him again.

"Hold on to it, buddy!" Paul shouted. Dan succeeded in catching the branch, but Paul's sense of relief didn't last long. He braced himself and pulled back and up, like he was hauling in a fish.

The brittle branch broke with a loud crack. Dan's eyes met his brother's with a quick glance filled with panic and defeat.

The unexpected loss of Dan's weight caused Paul to lose his balance and crash to the ground. Rising quickly, he discarded the broken half of the branch as if it were a spear. He resumed pacing, his mind focused on devising Plan C.

"Paul, go away! Scram out of here before they catch you," Dan pleaded.

"Shut up!" Paul snapped back. "I'm staying!"

"Leave me —"

"Stop trying to be noble! You're not good at it!" Paul jabbed his index finger at Dan. "You're coming with me, my dear brother, like it or not! Pipe down and let me figure something out. Hang on."

"To what!" Dan yelled.

Paul looked around the area, his mind racing with countless chaotic ideas barging into each other, none leading to a solution. Then he spotted a possibility.

One lower branch of another tree extended from the trunk in an arc over the quicksand. Although the limb looked dead and carried no leaves, it appeared more sturdy than the one he had just tried. It might be too high up to be of use, but...

"This time," Paul said to himself. But first, he had to discover if the limb would support him.

Approaching the tree, he reached out and gripped the limb. He lifted his feet off the soft earth, letting his full weight dangle from the branch. The wood creaked, but held firm, reassuring him of its strength as he hung there, suspended above the ground.

Dropping back to the dirt, Paul rubbed his hands together and took a deep breath as he got ready. His whole idea screamed danger and stupidity, but he was out of options. His brother's life depended on him.

Paul leaped once more, wrapping both arms around the bark of the limb. Grunting with exertion, he hoisted himself on top of the branch. It quivered under his weight, swaying precariously.

"Dan, hang on!" Paul said again, his voice sharp. "Here come the Marines!"

Paul gripped the wood. As he looked down the branch's length, it appeared to narrow almost to the thinness of a high wire strung over the center ring at a circus. And in this performance, the net underneath was deadly.

He had no choice but to crawl along the limb, so he started, the branch trembling with each movement. Or maybe it was he who was trembling. He couldn't tell which.

Dan watched from below, a reminder to Paul of why he couldn't fall. Both of them flailing in the quicksand would be a permanent end to the Case twins' adventures.

The tree shuddered with a kind of malevolent menace, as if planning to fling Paul off like a horse does with an unwanted rider. He clamped his legs around the branch, imagining he could strengthen the wood through sheer willpower alone.

He continued to creep along the limb. As he moved, a slick sheen of sweat glossed his palms and blurred his grip, every nerve in his body keyed to the possibility of slipping.

A more violent tremor passed through the wood as Dan went on, a giant shrug that threatened to unseat him. He clung tight, legs vised and knotted, keeping him in a tense, precarious balance.

"Ready or not, here I come," Dan said, but his attempt at a light tone failed and was wholly unconvincing.

He shimmied his way along the rough surface. The limb swayed beneath his weight, dipping and bobbing like a ship on a restless sea. Time stretched as endlessly as the last day of school before Paul arrived where he wanted, peering down at his brother.

Paul clung to the branch, wrapping his legs around it as tightly as possible. He locked one arm around it for stability and extended his other arm downward toward Dan, his fingers spread wide.

He leaned down more, the strain evident in his tight muscles, his torso extending until the gap between their hands was reduced to mere inches. "Alright, buddy. Grab hold! Come on!"

The limb dipped down about an inch, a warning of how unstable Paul's perch truly was. He channeled every ounce of his energy, strength, and will into what he was doing, the tension vibrating through him as if he were a coiled spring. Beads of sweat trickled down his face as he inched downward, lowering his body with care. With each movement, the branch vibrated.

Dan reached up. The twins' fingertips brushed.

"Come on, Dan, grab!" Paul said, his voice cracking with effort. "Try, buddy, try!"

Paul's muscles burned and quivered, yet he stretched harder, forcing everything he had into the task. The gap between the brothers appeared huge, but Paul edged closer, his fingers straining for contact. His feet dug into the scratchy bark, and he shifted his position, anchoring himself on the swaying limb. It shivered beneath him, but he ignored the tremors, focusing solely on reaching his brother.

Paul's hands latched onto Dan's. Dan's grip strengthened, almost as if he were trying to prove how strong he was. A worrying thought flickered through Paul: could the branch support their combined weight, or would it snap?

The twins' faces contorted, muscles straining as pain and effort crossed their faces. Paul tried to pull Dan up, every sinew in his arms taut and his biceps bulging, but his twin remained stubbornly stuck in the quicksand, barely shifting despite Paul's efforts.

"Push with your legs!" Paul grunted out through clenched teeth. "Kick your feet! See if you can wriggle free! Do something!"

"I'm trying to pull my knees up and push down." Dan's movements rippled through Paul as he wrestled against the heavy tug of the quicksand. "Wait! I think that's working! It seems to be getting looser."

"Then keep doing what you're doing!" Paul said. "Keep it up, Dan! Don't stop!"

Paul shifted, adjusting his position to wedge his weight more securely along the gnarled bark of the branch. Its surface scratched his chest and stomach. He felt rather than heard a crack as the limb quivered beneath him. He focused on his brother, who tightened his grip on his hand, his knuckles whitening with the effort. Their eyes locked, and Paul saw a vow from Dan — a refusal to surrender, no matter what.

Dan's body twisted and jerked as he struggled to free himself. Paul thought the grip of the quicksand shifted, loosened a little. Dan kept writhing and battling against the dense, sticky muck. With every painful inch, he gained release from the quicksand's relentless tug. Paul tightened his hold, pushing his limits, determined not to lose his grasp on his twin. Dan's shoulders moved away from the quicksand and closer to his brother.

"Keep doing what you're doing, buddy! You're getting there!" Paul's words spilled out in a pressured rush. The branch wobbled beneath him. Paul's muscles were both numb and ablaze with pain, and he fought the urge to cry out.

Dan jerked up with renewed energy, the push of his legs combined with the strength of his determination. He released one hand and grabbed Paul's wrist, then did the same with the other one.

"You're doing great, Dan! Stay at it!" Paul encouraged. "Work your way up my arm! Like it was a rope!"

Dan gritted his teeth and struggled again. He made crucial more inches, and his upper body became free of the quicksand's grasp. Paul's position was both awkward and painful, the limb turning into a rigid knife pressing on his ribs and stomach as Dan's weight pulled down on him. But he would not let go.

Slowly, hand over hand, Dan hauled himself out of the mire. Paul winced in pain, his arm feeling like it was being wrenched out of its socket, and the branch about to slice him in half. With a final, powerful heave, Dan clamped his hands around the limb. He hauled his feet out of the muck, gasping and wild-eyed, a triumphant grin spreading across his face.

"You did it, Danny boy! You did it!" Paul said.

A loud crack sounded.

The branch quaked under the brothers' combined weight and dropped an inch, sending a shiver through Paul's bones and his confidence. In a reflex, he locked down harder with his legs, fighting the limb's movements that threatened to dump them into the quicksand.

"We've overloaded this branch. It may not hold both of us much longer," Paul said. "I need to jump off. Can you get back to dry land on your own?"

"No sweat," Dan said. "Just move out of my way, my dear brother."

"I don't even know why I bothered to ask," Paul said with a smirk.

Paul inched backward along the limb, his breath coming in nervous spurts. His hands gripped the bark tightly while he tried to ignore the way the branch wobbled under him. The wood protested with a series of ominous creaks and groans, as if warning him of its impending failure. He began wondering if the limb had somehow grown in length after he climbed on since it seemed to take more time to back off it, but finally, his feet met the reassuring, solid tree trunk.

He let out a huge sigh of relief as he dropped off the limb, his shoes thumping onto the ground. Rotating and stretching his shoulders, he looked at his brother. Now, that branch needed to hold just a little longer...

Dan pulled himself up with a grunt, hoisting his legs into the air and locking his ankles around the branch above him. He dangled upside down, looking like a sloth clinging to its perch. Inch by inch, he shuffled along the limb. It groaned under his shifting weight, the wood creaking threats.

Eyes fixed on the ground where Paul waited, Dan continued. Reaching the spot directly next to his brother, Dan took a deep breath. With a swift and fluid motion, he released his hold, executing a nimble dismount to land on the grassy earth beside Paul.

"Ta-da! What a cinch!" Dan spread his arms like a circus performer taking a bow. "We're even. Two saves each. No, wait..." He counted on his fingers. "Two for me and one for you."

"Okay, okay, I owe you one," Paul laughed.

"Then you have dirty dishes duty at home forever," Dan said.

"Well, let's not get crazy about it." Paul grinned. "Maybe every other month."

"Good. That'll also spare Mom and me from eating what you call 'cooking' sometimes," Dan replied.

"Come on. I found the vehicles... a car and a truck. Let's go. We need to blow outta here," Paul said.

With Paul in the lead, the twins crashed through the underbrush, pushing aside branches and brush.

"You said there's a car and a truck?" Dan asked between heavy breaths.

"Yeah." Paul ducked under a low-hanging branch. "Not far now."

The brothers pushed forward with renewed energy, the promise of escape driving them on.

"There!" Paul pointed ahead where the forest started to thin.

They burst from the forest's edge onto the hard-packed dirt road. The vehicles sat where Paul had found them — both the Buick Roadmaster and the truck.

"See? We have a choice." Paul glanced at Dan. "Okay, which one?"

Dan charged forward. "Whichever one we can nab."

They ran the last several yards, first Dan, then Paul, stopping next to the Roadmaster.

Paul examined the car, catching his breath as Dan caught his. "Nice car. The Professor's, you think?"

"Who else?" Dan wiped the sweat from his forehead.

"Looks new." Paul stood and cupped his hands around his eyes to peer inside.

"He probably paid cash with bills that still had wet ink." Dan pulled the door handle. "Locked." He planted his fists on his waist and threw out a complaint. "Why would the Professor do that? Who would steal his car way out here?"

Paul lifted his eyebrows and slouched into a grin. "We would."

Dan gave an exasperated sigh. He threw his hands up. "All right, all right. One down, one to go. Let's see if we have better luck with the truck."

They ran to it, parked a few yards away. Dan went straight for the driver's side and yanked on the door. He opened it for Paul to see. "Unlocked."

"Better than the last one," Paul said.

Dan swung the door wide and climbed in. He glanced at the dashboard. No keys dangled from the ignition switch. He gripped the steering wheel and tried not to scream in anger. He faced Paul and let go with an accusation. "Where are the keys?"

"How would I know?" Paul fired back.

"Didn't you check?" Dan demanded.

"No, I didn't." Paul crossed his arms across his chest. "It seems I heard a plaintive cry for help that distracted me."

Dan gave a sheepish grin. "Sorry."

Paul pointed. "Look in the glove compartment."

Dan popped it open. Empty except for a crumpled map and an ancient pack of cigarettes. He shut the compartment with a "bah."

He swept his hands along the dashboard, searching every crevice. His fingers probed the narrow gap between the worn-out seats. Moving to the sun visors, he flipped them down, then slapped them back up when they didn't have anything hidden behind them.

"I guess no keys. What now?" Paul asked.

"I'll hotwire it," Dan answered after a moment's pause.

The skepticism was clear in Paul's voice. "Have you been living a secret life I didn't know about? How do you know how to do something like that?"

"Well," Dan drawled out, "I read about it in a mystery magazine detective story. It's simple. You... ah... grab some wires under the dashboard and... ah... twist them together... or something like that." He reached under the dash. "I think one of these is —"

"We don't have the time for on-the-job training!" Paul spat out.

"Have you got a better idea, bright boy?" Dan fired back.

Paul thought for a second. "Yeah! Remember what happened to us at the Maitland Mansion?"

Dan gave a snort. "A lot of things happened to us in that crazy place."

"No, no! The cars! Remember? You wanted to drive to get help, but —" Paul gestured for Dan to finish.

Dan got it and sat up straight. "I couldn't because Dietz disabled all the cars!"

Paul nodded. "Exactly. So if we can't use these," he tapped the truck and pointed to the Roadmaster, "we'll fix them, so the gang can't either! You know, so they can't start the car or the truck!"

"Pull out the spark plug wires! And the distributor cap!" Dan picked up eagerly. "We'll toss them in the swamp where they'll never find them, then take off down the road. It must meet up with a highway somewhere down the line. From there, we can hitch a ride."

"My dear brother, you should get sucked into quicksand more often. It squeezed the brain cells out of your feet and into your head."

Dan slid out of the truck's driver's seat, softly closing the door. He pointed to the hood. "I'll start with —"

"Wait!" Paul grabbed Dan's arm. He whispered, "Listen!"

The sound of two voices approached. And they were getting closer.

Chapter Fourteen

Paul glanced over his shoulder. "The animals have escaped from their cages."

He got down quickly, knees hitting the dirt with a soft thud, and waved to Dan. His finger jabbed toward the shadowy space under the truck. With his hand, he mimicked the scuttling motion of a crab, urging Dan to hurry. Understanding the command, Dan nodded, climbed out of the cab, and softly closed the door. He dropped to the dirt.

Dan pressed his body flat against the ground, crawling under the truck's chassis, with Paul close on his heels. The twins came out on the opposite side, crouching over as they hurried toward the road's edge. They hid themselves behind a dense patch of swamp brush, their feet sinking slightly into the boggy soil.

The voices got louder, stopping on the far side of the truck.

"So you have the address of the new location?" It was the Professor's voice.

"Yeah," came the reply from Rocky. "What about those kids?"

"I will have to give them credit for their cleverness," the Professor said. "It is something to be admired... but not too much. I am sure they have fled the area by now."

"What makes you think that?" Rocky sounded incredulous.

"Do think about it, Rocky. They would be fools to remain around here after locking us in the attic," the Professor said. "Why would they stay? The two most likely escaped into the marshes, which means the swamp may do our work for us. Or at the very least, they will be lost for quite a while until they find help. If they discovered this road, it is miles before it joins the highway. But remember, all the turns and other roads between. One wrong turn, and again, they are wandering in the wilds for hours. Plenty of time for us to drive to our new headquarters."

"If you thought those kids escaped, why did you order the search for them?" Rocky asked.

"It is simple psychology, dear boy. The others were angry and embarrassed at the boys' trick. Giving them something to do allows them to burn off their energy. To feel as if they are accomplishing something," the Professor said. The sound of a car door unlocking came through the air. "Of course, they are not."

"Oh, okay." After a moment's pause, Rocky spoke again, the student trying one last time to trip up his teacher. "So what do we do if we do find them?"

The car door opened, and the Professor sighed. "In that highly unlikely situation, Rocky, you have my permission to eliminate them in any manner you desire. You can stretch the process out as long as you wish to accomplish that. It's 4:30 now. I will expect you at our new location by eight tonight."

"Okay, but I'm gonna to switch the license plates on the truck first," Rocky said. "If those two passed here, they may have memorized the numbers. They're smart enough. The truck isn't as fast as your car. If they call the police, they'll probably catch the truck more easily than your car."

"Commendably cautious, Rocky," the Professor said. "Give the others another twenty minutes to search, then leave."

"Right. Meet you at the new headquarters," Rocky said. "Eight pm on the dot."

Dan carefully raised his head above the thick foliage. Through the leaves, he saw the Professor slide into the sleek Roadmaster. The car's engine roared to life, a deep rumble that seemed to vibrate through the swampy ground beneath them. With a spray of gravel, the Professor accelerated away, the sound of the powerful motor fading as the vehicle disappeared down the winding road.

Paul tapped Dan and placed his mouth close to his brother's ear. "Are they gone?"

"The Professor's left, but Rocky's still here." Dan kept his eyes fixed on the huge man now moving toward the back of the truck.

Rocky opened the canvas flaps at the truck's rear and climbed inside. He emerged moments later with a screwdriver clutched in one hand and two shiny license plates in the other. He knelt behind the truck and began unscrewing the current plates.

"What's he doing?" Paul asked, squinting through the brush.

"Switching the plates, like he said he would," Dan replied quietly. "Good move. It wouldn't have mattered if we had reported the license number..."

"Because it's different now," Paul finished.

They watched in silence as Rocky completed attaching the new plates. He gathered the old ones along with the screwdriver and returned everything to the truck bed. After shutting the flaps like curtains, he brushed off his hands. He checked the area with a quick glance, then headed back in the direction of the mill. Neither twin moved until Rocky was out of sight.

"At least now we know their plan," Dan said, rising to his feet. "They're moving to a different headquarters tonight."

"And they think we've either escaped through the swamp or we're lost on some back goat track." Paul stood up beside him, brushing dirt from his knees. "So what do we do now? Should we actually do what the Professor thinks we did?" He jerked his thumb behind him. "Try to escape through the swamp or head up the road? We've got at least a twenty-minute head start."

Dan shook his head and gestured toward the dense, murky wilderness beyond the road's edge. "I don't fancy trying to fight through that swamp, or being stuck out there all night. More quicksand, more snakes, more who knows what else. Plus, we'd be soaking wet at once. Let's not tempt hypothermia, even in this heat."

Paul waved down the dirt road, cutting through swampland. "Well, that way isn't much better. If the Professor was right, it's miles before we hit anything resembling civilization. And we don't know which turns to take." He shrugged. "I suppose we could always hide here until they leave, and hope they don't find us... We could spend the night at the mill after they go."

Dan paced a few steps and shook his head. "We need to think in a different way. The Professor believed we ran. He was positive we had left. Said we'd be fools if we hadn't." He stopped and looked at his brother. "So what if we acted like fools?"

"I don't follow..." Paul's brow furrowed.

"They expected us to take off... they think we did," Dan said. "So we'll do the opposite. Sometimes the safest place to hide is right under their noses." He nodded toward the truck. "If we could somehow hitch a ride without being seen —"

Paul glanced between the truck and his brother. An expression of disbelief spread across his face. "What a minute! You're not suggesting that we hitch a ride *with* them, are you?"

"That's the general idea, my dear brother." Dan went to the back of the truck, Paul following.

"You're crazy!" Paul said. "Screwy, nutso, batty, off your rocker... We'd be trapped back there."

"Not trapped," Dan corrected. "Hiding in plain sight. Like stowaways."

"Stowaways get thrown overboard when they're discovered, buddy boy," Paul fired back.

"It's a chance we'll have to take. The gang would never think to search here, would have no reason to, so they won't." Dan peeked through the flaps and into the bed. It was filled with press components, boxes, and other items hidden beneath a tarp. He turned back to Paul. "Probably."

Paul groaned.

"We hide ourselves back there. When the truck stops, like to gas up, or at a signal... when it slows driving through a town, something like that, we bail out. With us raising a stink and other people around, Rocky and his friends wouldn't dare come after us. They'll take off. And we could get the cops after them, too. You said the Case twins have faced down gangsters, arsonists and kidnappers. Time to add counterfeiters to that list," said Dan.

The sound of rustling foliage and snapping twigs reached their ears from the forest, along with the murmur of voices and rustling of branches. Multiple sets of feet were heading their way.

"They're coming back now," Dan whispered urgently.

Paul's eyes widened as he looked in the direction of the sound. "That wasn't twenty minutes! Wasn't even five!"

"Quick decision time." Dan gestured toward the back of the truck. "In or out?"

Paul glared at his twin, his face a mixture of frustration, anger and resignation. "I oughta have my head examined for listening to my dumb brother," he growled, but he was already moving. With one fluid motion, he pulled himself up and slipped through the canvas flaps into the bed.

Dan scrambled behind him. Paul was making his way to the very back, behind the pieces of the press and other boxes. When Dan joined him, they both squeezed into the cramped space between cardboard boxes filled with bundles of counterfeit money and the truck's cab. Paul yanked the tarp over them just in time, as the voices became clear enough to understand.

"I'm telling you, they're lucky I didn't find them," Tommy was grumbling. "If I'd caught those two, I would've taught them a lesson they'd never forget. Nobody makes —"

" — makes a fool of you," Vic cut in, his voice sharp with irritation. "We know. You said that a million times. Now shut up."

Tommy fell silent, but Dan imagined the sullen look on his face. The twins exchanged glances in the dim light filtering through the tarp.

"Vic, you drive, and I'll take shotgun," Rocky said. "Tommy and Mousey ride in the back."

"The back? Three can sit in the cab," Tommy protested. "Why can't Mousey ride in the back by himself?"

"Because I said so." Rocky's tone left no room for argument. "Now get in."

Dan's stomach dropped. His plan had gotten much more complicated. A punch in the arm came from Paul. An "I told you this was a bad idea" slug if there ever was one.

The truck's rear flaps were yanked open, flooding the inside portion with late afternoon light. The twins pressed themselves deeper into their hiding spot, barely daring to breathe. The truck jiggled a little as two bodies climbed aboard.

"This stinks," Tommy complained. He settled against what sounded like the wooden slats that ran down two sides of the bed. "I don't see why I gotta ride back here. It's like I'm cattle."

"At least we're getting out of this swamp," Mousey said.

The canvas flaps dropped back into place, enveloping the truck bed in dim light again. Dan heard Tommy and Mousey moving about, getting comfortable amid the load. The cab's front doors swung open, and the seats creaked as Rocky and Vic climbed in, then the doors closed with a resounding, metallic thud.

The truck's engine roared to life, and the vehicle lurched forward, throwing the twins against each other. The uneven dirt road made for a bumpy ride, and Dan had to brace himself to keep from making any noise.

"I wonder where this new place is," Mousey asked over the rumble of the motor and the creaking of the truck.

"The Professor told me." Tommy's voice rang with pride. He continued as though he were in the Professor's complete confidence. "Some old warehouse outside Clayton. He tells me it's perfect — no nosy neighbors, plenty of room for the press."

"How long to get there?"

"A few hours, I think."

Dan groaned inside. Stuck for a long time in the back with these two lugs was not his idea of a fun time. The brothers were crammed in a small, uncomfortable space. He wondered how his muscles would protest being confined in one position for so long.

"We should've stayed back at the mill," Mousey said. "Those two are gone by now."

"The Professor says he wants us all at the new place tonight," Tommy declared. "And that's good enough for me. Anyway, I was getting tired of that old mill. It gave me the creeps at night."

Tommy and Mousey fell silent. The cargo shifted with a soft rustle, boxes jostling against one another, creating a rhythmic whisper that mingled with the gentle flapping of the canvas cover as it snapped along the wooden stakes of the bed. Beneath it all, the steady growl of the engine throbbed through the vehicle, a constant rumble that vibrated through the metal frame as the truck bounced down the rough road.

Dan chanced a peek. He lifted the edge of the tarp enough to see what was going on around him. Tommy sat at the end of the bed by the flaps, his posture rigid and tense. His arms were crossed tightly over his chest, and the brim of his faded cap was pulled down, casting a shadow over his eyes. Sitting across from Tommy, Mousey was absorbed in a well-worn comic book with frayed edges and dog-eared pages, his fingers tracing the colorful illustrations as he read.

Following a stop, the truck turned and picked up speed on what seemed like smoother pavement. Dan assumed they were now on the highway. When the truck either slowed down or came to a halt, the brothers would make a break for it, ready to battle Tommy and Mousey if needed, to make their escape.

Mile after uneventful mile rolled by, and doubt crept into Dan's mind. Had he made a mistake? Should they have stayed at the mill? He couldn't shake the worry that the gang might not stop along the route. Paul's warning echoed in Dan's brain — what if his brother was right? Should they have simply stayed at the mill and figured something out in the morning? The twins could end up trapped at the gang's new headquarters. But again, maybe, just maybe, this was their only chance — not only of escaping, but of rounding up the gang for Ricardo. Perhaps even staying alive. Uncertainty gnawed at him, yanking him in different directions.

Talk from the cab pulled Dan from his thoughts. He tensed, wondering if this might be their time to escape.

"Take it easy, Vic," Rocky rumbled from the front seat. "There's a cop ahead."

"Where?" Vic asked, his voice tight with concern. "I don't see any."

"Over on the right — parked by that drive-in hamburger joint," Rocky said.

"Man, Rocky, you've got good eyes," Vic said. "I can't see him. That stand is way in the distance."

Rocky chuckled, a low, gravelly sound. "I didn't need to lay eyes on him, Vic. I can smell 'em from miles away. Make sure you're doin' the speed limit on the dot. We can't afford to be pulled over for a ticket."

Dan felt Paul's elbow dig into his ribs. This could be their opportunity. If the truck slowed down enough while passing the hamburger stand, they might be able to jump out without hurting themselves. The presence of a police officer nearby would be perfect — the gang wouldn't dare pursue them in that case.

"Tommy, Mousey — stay quiet back there," Rocky called through the small rear window of the cab. "We're passin' a cop."

"Got it, Rocky," Tommy answered. He sat up straighter.

Mousey folded his comic book and shoved it into his jacket pocket. "Think we should check the load? Make sure nothing shifts?"

"Nah, just sit tight," Tommy replied. "Less movement, the better."

Dan's heart sank. Their guards were now fully vigilant. He caught Paul's eye in the dim light, seeing his own disappointment reflected in it. This chance was slipping away.

The truck slowed and then maintained its reduced speed.

"Nice and easy, Vic. How fast are you goin'?" Rocky said from the front.

"The limit on the nose."

"Okay. We're comin' up on him now," Rocky said. "We'll cruise on by."

Dan's mind raced. The police officer was ahead — their perfect opportunity for escape — but Tommy and Mousey were too alert. He needed some way to send a message.

A box of counterfeits pressed against his side. Dan glanced at it, then at the gap along the wooden slats and canvas cover of the bed. An idea formed.

With careful movements, Dan eased his hand into the box, feeling the crisp edges of the fake currency. He grabbed a thick handful, sliding the bills between his fingers.

"Almost there," Vic said. "I'll slow a little more. Be under the limit, then there's no chance of him noticing."

"Good thinkin'," Rocky said.

Moving with agonizing slowness to avoid rustling the tarp, Dan inched his hand toward the side of the truck. He found a narrow gap where the canvas cover met the wooden stake bed. The fabric wasn't pulled completely taut, leaving just enough space.

Dan pushed his hand through the opening, the rush of air blowing against his fingers. The truck was slower now as it neared the hamburger stand where the police car sat. Perfect timing.

"Look at the cop. Stuffing the burger into his fat face," Rocky chuckled.

Dan released the first bill, feeling it flutter away into the slipstream. Then another. And another. Soon, a stream of counterfeit twenties and fifties was flying from his hand, dancing behind the truck.

The seat crunched as Rocky settled back into it. "We're past him now. Wait until we get around that bend before you speed up. I'm gonna catch a little shuteye."

"Right," Vic said.

The truck rumbled on. And nothing happened.

Dan's stomach churned with anxiety as he wondered if the policeman had spotted the fluttering fake currency. He banked on the fact that it had caught the officer's eye, so the police would pull them over. But that didn't seem to have been the result. It looked like his idea was a complete failure. Just as he was beginning to lose hope, Vic spoke up.

"Uh, Rocky?" Vic's voice was tight. "Wake up. We've got company."

Rocky grunted. "What is it?"

"The cop's behind us," Vic said. "He must have pulled out of the hamburger joint."

"What's he doing?" Rocky asked.

"Nothing much. Only... following." Vic paused, perhaps glancing in the rearview mirror. "He's staying about four or five car lengths back."

"Could be nothin'," Rocky said, though his tone suggested otherwise. "This may be part of his regular beat. Keep your cool, Vic. Watch your drivin'. Stay exactly at the speed limit — not over, not under. Nothin' that looks suspicious."

"Right, right," Vic replied.

Tommy leaned toward the cab. "What's going on?"

"Shut up," Rocky said. "Cop's tailing us."

The truck maintained its steady pace, the tension growing inside the vehicle. Dan felt Paul's grip tighten on his arm. Dan grinned and reached into the box of fake bills again. The policeman was following. His plan had worked! But now they were trapped in the back with Tommy and Mousey. Time for another sprinkling of funny money to catch the cop's attention once more.

Rocky shifted in his seat. The passenger side window slid down, and the outside mirror made a small squeak. Rocky must have angled it differently. "I'm keepin' an eye on him. Don't look back, Vic. Act natural."

Dan stopped. The re-aimed mirror now may show a direct reflection along the truck bed, offering Rocky a glimpse of the canvas covering the cargo area. In this new position, the mirror would clearly show the scattering of the counterfeit bills. Dan let go of the cash and took his hand from the box.

"If we're pulled over, we're cooked," Mousey said in a panicked whisper. "The Professor's gonna kill us if we get caught. We'll go to jail. I don't wanna go to jail."

"Calm down and shut up," Tommy snapped.

"You think that cop spotted something?" Vic said.

"Maybe. Maybe not." Rocky's voice was controlled. "Just drive normal. If he wanted to pull us over, he'd have done it already."

The truck continued to rumble down the highway. Dan was pretzel-tense, hoping the cop would make a move and stop them, giving a chance for him and Paul to escape.

Vic spoke after a while. "He's still behind us."

"I can see that," Rocky said. "Make a right here. Let's see if he follows."

The truck slowed and made a turn onto another street. Dan braced himself against the boxes as they bounced over a gutter.

"He's turning too," Vic said, his voice rising in alarm.

"Calm down, Vic," Rocky ordered. "Maybe he's goin' this way, too. This road goes to Clayton as well."

Dan crossed his fingers. "Please, please, please..." he repeated in his mind.

More nerve-racking minutes as the truck lurched on.

Vic spoke up. "Wait... he's swinging off. To the left, off toward town."

"He's gone." Rocky chuckled. "Nothing behind us but that black sedan."

Dan struggled to keep himself from springing up and shouting, "What!" As the tension ebbed away, it left him torn between a heavy sense of defeat and a nagging feeling of helplessness.

The truck continued on, transporting the twins to their uncertain fate.

Chapter Fifteen

Every bump in the road felt like judgment to Dan, each jolt a reminder of his monumentally stupid idea. The truck's metal floor bit into his shoulder blades as he lay there, staring up at the canvas covering that trapped them inside this mobile coffin. Beside him, Paul's breathing came in shallow bursts, the only sound breaking the rumble of tires on asphalt.

Dan wanted to apologize to Paul. He now knew he should have listened to him, should have agreed to stay at the mill overnight. He believed he was outsmarting the situation by hitching a ride in the gang's truck. Now, caught in the result of his bad decision, he couldn't shake the feeling of guilt that clung to him, knowing he'd led them both... what was that saying? "Out of the frying pan, into the fire."

But a tiny part of him still held to the belief that his idea had a possibility it might work. Some way, somehow, the brothers would get out of this mess.

Stopping, the truck made a left turn. The road became rougher, not the smooth asphalt of the highway. The truck hit a pothole, sending Dan and Paul both an inch into the air before crashing back down. Pain shot through Dan's already bruised ribs. Paul gave a small gasp.

"Hey!" Tommy and Mousey protested.

"Watch where you're goin'!" Rocky complained.

"Sorry, fellas," Vic said.

After a few moments of just the engine grumbling, Vic spoke again.

"This place is as out of the way as the mill was."

"Yeah, the Professor knows his stuff. He's good at turnin' up places like this," Rocky replied. After a few minutes of silence, he said, "There it is, up ahead. The Professor said to... yeah, right there. See? The garage is open. Drive in there."

"Okay," Vic said.

The truck slowed to a crawl as it approached the destination, its tires crunching over gravel. With a sudden burst of acceleration, it gunned up a slight incline of the ramp. The motor roared, bouncing off walls, a sure sign they had entered the space of an inside garage. With a squeal of brakes, the truck came to a stop.

"End of the line!" Rocky called. "Everybody out!"

The truck rocked slightly as Rocky and Vic swung the heavy doors open and stepped down from the cab, the metallic clank of the doors reverberating in the still air. Tommy and Mousey climbed out of the truck bed, causing the canvas covering to flutter noisily. The loud rumbling clang of a metal door shutting echoed. Dan realized it was the garage door, sealing the brothers inside the building with the gang.

Dan's stomach knotted as he considered any options. If the gang left the garage, it might be the perfect moment for him and Paul to try their escape. But then, Rocky's next words smashed his hopes.

"You three go upstairs and talk with the Professor," Rocky said. "He'll tell you where he wants stuff. I'll change the plates again in case that cop took them down."

With a series of mumbled "rights", Dan listened as Vic, Tommy, and Mousey shuffled out of the garage, their footsteps sounding off the concrete floor. After a few moments, Rocky grasped the thick canvas flaps at the back of the truck, tugging them open with a swift motion. The fabric rustled loudly. With a grunt, Rocky climbed into the bed, the truck bouncing as he did.

Dan's muscles tightened as Rocky rifled through the cargo toward the back of the truck, muttering to himself. The tarp that covered the brothers from view shifted slightly as Rocky's hand brushed against it. Dan stopped breathing, his heart pounding in his chest like a frantic drum.

"Nah," Rocky grumbled under his breath. The sound of a box opening followed. "Not here."

Suddenly, the heavy tarp was yanked back, exposing the twins on the floor. Rocky's eyes widened in shock as he took in the sight. The canvas hung limply from his hand, forgotten, as he stood frozen, his gaze locked on the brothers.

"It's you two!" Rocky cried in astonishment.

Dan fumbled for what to say. "Surprise!" was all he could manage.

Rocky recovered quickly. Stepping back, he pulled his gun from his coat pocket and dropped the tarp. He carefully backed out of the bed to the garage floor, the revolver trained on Dan and Paul. "Alright, you guys, step out of there, real easy like. Keep your hands where I can see 'em."

Dan and Paul exchanged tense glances. Dan slowly rose from the floor, his hands raised high above his head, fingers splayed wide in surrender. Picking his way through the boxes, he climbed down to the garage floor. Paul mirrored Dan's actions and cautiously got out of the truck and stood next to his brother.

The garage was a cavernous space that could easily fit three trucks parked side by side. Impressive roll-down metal doors dominated one wall, their surfaces gleaming slightly under the overhead lights. On opposite sides, two doors stood, their frames sturdy and plain. In the center of the room, a large open manhole gaped like the mouth of a mysterious tunnel, its heavy cover resting askew on the floor, as if abandoned by a distracted workman. The air was tinged with the faint scent of motor oil and cold steel. The gang's truck was parked next to one wall.

"Face the wall, and spread 'em." Rocky jerked his gun in the direction he wanted the twins to go.

Dan and Paul obeyed, pressing themselves against the cold concrete block wall.

"I'm sorry," Dan whispered to his brother.

Paul returned a weak smile. "Well, at least I won't have to do the dishes now."

"Shut up!" Rocky barked. He raised his voice. "Professor! Professor! Come down here! It's important!"

"Yes, yes, what is it?" The Professor's reply came from upstairs. In a few moments, light, precise footsteps entered the garage. "What is the —" There was a moment's stunned silence. "I do not believe it."

"Believe it," Rocky said. He spoke to the brothers. "You two, turn around."

Dan and Paul did so. The Professor's eyebrows shot up, his mouth slightly agape as he shifted between surprise and a small smile hinting at admiration. The door creaked open, with Vic and Tommy entering. They took their places behind the Professor, astonishment on their faces.

"Found them hiding in the back of the truck," Rocky said.

The Professor folded his arms and stared at the twins. He shook his head. "I do not know if you two are the most clever young men I have ever encountered, or the most stupid."

"What do we do with them?" Rocky asked.

"Well, we most certainly cannot let them go. They have been most inconvenient as well." The Professor thought a moment. "Tie their hands in front of them and suspend them from that pipe near the ceiling. I will attend to these two myself. To repay them for all the trouble they have caused."

Tommy blanched and took a step back. "You mean like Washington?"

The Professor nodded. An evil smile spread across his lips. "Only I can take longer with these two. I have the time. They will be works of art. After all, we are far enough from the city that the screams would not disturb anyone."

"Except for us," Vic said under his breath.

A chill rang through Dan. He glanced at his brother. Paul glared at the Professor with steely defiance.

Mousey burst into the garage. "Professor! Professor! The cops!"

The Professor spun around. "What is that?"

"Cops! Cops!" Mousey stopped a second to catch his breath. He pointed. "I saw them from upstairs! A line of cars slowing on the highway, turning onto the road coming here!"

Fishing a gun from his coat pocket, the Professor handed it to Tommy. "You and Mousey keep an eye on these two. They might be of some use after all, as hostages. Rocky and Vic, come with me. We will assess the circumstances." The Professor, Vic and Rocky rushed from the room.

Tommy pointed the weapon at the twins, a cocky grin spreading on his face. "Come on. Make a move. I'd love to drill one of you. Trust me, it'll be a faster way to go than what the Professor has planned for you."

Mousey moved in frantic circles on the floor, his sneakers scuffing against the concrete with each urgent step. His fingers combed through his unruly curly hair, pulling at the strands. "The cops, the cops. We're cooked," he muttered, his voice a mix of panic and resignation. "It's over. I'm going to jail. Jail!" he whimpered, eyes darting around as if expecting police to materialize at any moment out of thin air.

"Stop squeaking, Mousey! Get hold of yourself!" Tommy barked.

Mousey's eyes darted wildly around the garage, his breath coming in rapid, shallow gasps. His small frame trembled as he let out a series of pitiful moans, a cornered and frightened creature. With each passing second, his steps quickened, the soles of his shoes scuffing frantically against the floor as he paced around and around, his anxiety mounting with every stride. Finally, he could take it no more.

"I'm getting out of here!" Mousey shouted. He bolted for the door opposite the one the Professor and the others took.

"Mousey, get back here!" Tommy yelled. His attention was distracted by the fleeing figure for a second.

That was all the time Paul needed.

Paul launched himself, his shoulder crashing into Tommy's midsection with all the force he could muster. The impact caused Tommy to gasp, "oof" in an almost comical manner. They both hurtled backward, colliding with the concrete wall with a sickening thud. Tommy's head whipped back and cracked against the unforgiving surface. The revolver flew from his hand.

The gun sailed through the air in a slow-motion arc, spinning as it reflected the harsh fluorescent lighting. Dan dove for it across the garage floor, his fingers stretching toward the tumbling weapon. His hand brushed the cold metal for just a heartbeat before it slipped from his grasp.

The pistol clattered against the concrete, skittering across the smooth surface with terrible momentum, straight toward the open manhole in the center of the room. As if aimed, it slid into the darkness below with a distant, echoing splash.

Dan stared in disbelief after the vanished weapon. "I couldn't have done that if I had tried."

Paul grabbed Tommy by the front of his shirt, pulling him away from the wall. With a swift, practiced motion, Paul delivered a powerful right cross to Tommy's jaw. Paul continued to hold on to Tommy's shirt even as the fabric tore with a loud rip, leaving Tommy sprawled on the ground with his shirt ripped open.

"Get Mousey!" Paul ordered. "I can take care of this one."

Dan dashed through the door that Mousey had passed through, entering a dim hallway resembling a long, narrow tunnel that spanned the entire length of the building. At the far end, he spotted Mousey, his small figure outlined against the dimming light from outside. He was frantically tugging at a stuck window, its paint-chipped frame resisting his attempts to open it. Dan ran toward him.

Mousey darted a frightened look over his shoulder at Dan. He gripped the window frame and, with a loud grunt, forced it open with a creak. He climbed through. Just moments later, Dan followed, squeezing through the narrow opening. Mousey was making a break for the woods that surrounded the warehouse.

***

Paul locked the door the gang had used and faced Tommy. "Get up. I told you it wasn't over between us. It's just you and me, pal."

With a sneer, Tommy got to his feet. He took off his torn shirt and tossed it aside. "Alright. Let's go, mug."

He swaggered in front of Paul, fists swinging loosely and wide, wearing an expression as if he'd already won. Paul, however, remained calm. He took the classic boxer's stance — hands up, elbows in, weight on the balls of his feet. His eyes focused solely on Tommy, studying his movements... planning, strategizing.

Paul knew, as a trained boxer, he had a strong edge due to his technique, control, and conditioning. Tommy was probably only a street fighter, but that could also mean he could be unpredictable and ruthless. Paul still believed he had the skills necessary to win, but he had to stay composed. To him, Tommy was just another opponent in the ring.

Tommy led off. He lunged forward with a wild haymaker that sliced through the air like a blade. It was a powerful attack but lacked control. Paul slipped under Tommy's swing with a swift ducking motion. He pivoted on his heel and fired back with a sharp jab straight to Tommy's nose. Enraged by this unexpected hit, Tommy charged at Paul like an untamed bull, his fists swinging wildly in a blur of fury.

Paul sidestepped just in time to avoid getting hit and countered with a body blow that sank deep into Tommy's stomach, folding him like a cheap pocketknife. Seizing the brief moment, Paul clinched onto Tommy tightly to halt his momentum and then shoved him off with controlled precision using both hands, creating distance between them again.

His face twisted in anger, Tommy tried again. He feinted left and then threw a looping right aimed at Paul's head. But Paul read it perfectly. He ducked under the punch again and stepped inside Tommy's guard before firing off a clean left hook that landed flush on Tommy's jaw, sending him stumbling backward, a dazed look in his eyes.

Paul moved forward slowly. His eyes remained sharp, his footwork tight and calculated. Tommy, now realizing he was outclassed, threw a wild punch out of nowhere. Paul was ready. He blocked it with his forearm, stepped inside Tommy's guard once more, and unleashed a crisp one-two combo that landed perfectly. The final uppercut from Paul snapped Tommy's head back like a whip cracking in the air. Unable to maintain balance any longer, Tommy's eyes glazed over, and he crumpled to the floor, out cold.

Paul shook out his hands and took a moment to steady his breathing. He was as calm and composed in victory as he was at the start of the fight. He addressed the figure prone on the ground. "Yeah, nobody makes a fool out of you, Tommy."

He heard more voices and commands coming from the other side of the door, likely from the police. Stepping over, he unlocked and opened the door. "There's one more in here, officers," he called out,

***

Dan sped up and tackled Mousey, sending them both tumbling to the ground. They rolled around in the dirt until Dan hauled

Mousey to his feet, restraining him with his arms pinned behind his back.

"Let me go! Let me go!" Mousey yelled. He thrashed against Dan's grip like a wild beast.

"Not a chance. You need to talk to the cops. You're a witness," Dan said.

"No!" Then all at once, Mousey's body went limp in Dan's grip. His shoulders slumped, and a choked sob escaped his throat. Tears welled up in his eyes and spilled down his dirt-streaked face.

"Look, I'll talk to the cops. Try to make it easy on you, but you were involved," Dan said.

"I want my Ma," Mousey moaned. "I wanna go home."

Dan loosened his hold slightly, surprised by the sudden change. "What?"

"I want my Ma," Mousey pleaded.

"Your Ma? Why? I thought the gang was your family now."

Mousey shook his head. "Ma and I had a fight. A big one." He sniffled loudly. "I called her names. Terrible names. Then I ran away, ran into Rocky, and we talked. I told him I could take care of the printing press. I like doing stuff like that. Been with the gang almost four weeks now."

"So you have a home? A real home?" Dan asked, his grip relaxing further.

Mousey nodded miserably. "A little place. Maybe not the nicest, but... I wanna tell Ma I'm sorry. Tell her she was right." A fresh wave of tears spilled down his cheeks. "I wanna go home. Mr. Watson at the garage down the street said he'd teach me how to fix cars after school. That's what I really want to do, you know? I like machines. I like working on them." He sniffed. "I couldn't leave the gang. I was afraid of Rocky."

Dan thought about what Mousey said, searching for any sign of lying just to get out of trouble. All he saw was a frightened kid who'd made a terrible mistake.

"Does the gang know your real name?" Dan asked.

Mousey shook his head. "No. Nobody knows. Not even the Professor. They just call me Mousey 'cause I'm small." He sniffed again. "I'm really Edgar. Edgar Norris."

"Do they know where you live?"

"No."

Dan recalled Mousey mentioning that the pipe was almost entirely rusted through when Mousey had tied him to it. Mousey tried to help Dan. Maybe it was time to repay the gesture. His voice softened. "How long would it take you to get home from here, Edgar?"

"Two days, maybe?" Mousey said, still sniffling. "If I catch rides and don't stop much."

"Go on, Edgar." Dan released Mousey, allowing his arms to drop to his sides. He stepped back. "Run. Get out of here. Go home to your mother."

Mousey spun around and looked at Dan. He wiped his eyes with his fists. "You're letting me go?"

Dan thought about how his parents had fled Chicago and Rizzo's gang to start a new life. "Everyone deserves a second chance.

Especially someone who knows they made a mistake." He pointed at Mousey. "Don't waste it."

Mousey stood frozen for a moment, as if unable to believe his luck. Then a smile broke through his tears. "Thank you... bless you... thank you... I won't forget this. Never ever. Thank you."

"Just learn to fix those cars," Dan called as Mousey backed away. "Now clear out!"

Mousey nodded vigorously, then turned and sprinted toward the tree line. He paused at the edge of the woods, gave Dan a final wave, and disappeared into the shadows. Dan watched the small figure melt into the trees, his silhouette melting into the shadows until there was nothing left but the rustling of leaves.

He let out a long breath, wondering if he'd made the right choice. Mousey deserved a chance to fix his life. Sometimes, that's all anyone needed — a way back home. After a few moments, a voice came from behind him.

"Halt! Put your hands up and turn around!"

The sharp command cut through the air. Dan's heart lurched in his chest as he slowly raised his hands skyward, palms open. He turned, muscles tensed, preparing to face one of the Professor's men. Instead, he found himself staring down the barrel of a police-issued revolver. Behind it stood Ricardo, his familiar face twisted in concentration until recognition dawned.

"Dan? Is that you? Or is it Paul?" Ricardo lowered his gun, disbelief etched across his features. The weapon hung loosely at his side as he blinked rapidly, as if trying to confirm what his eyes were telling him.

"Dan, live and in person. Paul's inside," Dan said, nodding toward the warehouse. He lowered his hands.

Ricardo put his gun into his shoulder holster with a shake of his head. "Why am I not surprised that you two are here?" His tone was a mixture of exasperation and grudging admiration.

Dan shrugged, offering no explanation.

A sudden rustling came from the bushes in the forest — a frantic, scurrying sound that made Ricardo tense again, his hand moving instinctively back toward his holster.

"What's that?" he asked, eyes narrowing as he scanned the trees.

Dan's lips curved into a faint smile. "Only a mouse."

Chapter Sixteen

Hours of statements and questions had wrung all the words out of Dan and Paul, leaving them bleary and tired. They sat side by side in the conference room at the Clayton Police Department. The officers let the brothers take a shower, then rustled up some T-shirts for them to wear. Dan and Paul were now proclaimed as members of the department's Youth Baseball Team.

Roberto rushed out and brought the twins some food after he found out they hadn't eaten all day. Now the two held cups of coffee, letting the welcome heat seep into their hands. The scent of the burgers and onions still lingered in the air.

Paul broke the silence with a weary sigh. "Well, it's been quite a day, my dear brother."

Dan turned, his eyes thick with exhaustion. "You can say that again."

Paul gave a weary sigh. "Well, it's been quite—" he started again.

Dan sat up straight. "Don't you dare!"

A few minutes of silence passed.

"Why is it always us?" Dan asked, staring at the floor. "Why do we always get caught up in such crazy things?"

"Must be the luck of the Irish, I guess," his brother answered.

Dan leaned toward his twin. "We're not Irish."

Paul shrugged. "Then that can't be the reason."

The two blew on their coffees.

"This stuff is burning hot." Paul glanced up at the clock on the wall. It reminded him of the one he spent hours staring at in his old math classroom, where he was positive time slowed down. "Two in the morning. Mom should be here soon."

Dan nodded. "Yeah."

"What did she say again?" Paul asked.

"After she found out we were okay, she said, 'We'd have a talk.'" Dan glanced at his brother. They both knew what that meant.

"Uh-oh," Paul groaned. He took a sip of coffee. "Blah. I forgot to add sugar." He searched around for the small packets that lay neglected on the table. He grabbed four, tore them open and dumped the white crystals into his cup.

Dan watched Paul with mild disgust. "I still have no idea how you can drink it that sweet."

"Matches my personality. How can you drink it that bitter?" Paul countered, stirring the sludge in his cup. Dan rolled his eyes.

A commotion erupted in the hallway — shuffling feet, the metallic jingle of handcuffs, and gruff voices giving directions.

The brothers turned toward the noise. Through the conference room's glass windows that faced the corridor, they watched as Rocky shuffled past first, his massive frame diminished somehow by the officers flanking him. With a scowl twisting his face, his eyes fixed on the floor.

Vic followed with a bored expression, as if this was just another day at the office. He yawned as he walked by.

Tommy came next, looking even younger than his years. His usual smug, cocky expression on his face was wiped clean, replaced by one of fear. He kept mumbling something to the federal agent, who was guiding him forward with a firm hand on his shoulder.

The Professor came last. He glimpsed the brothers through the window. Halting, he resisted the pushing from the officer behind him. Facing Dan and Paul, the Professor clicked his heels together and gave a respectful bow. The accompanying officer got him to continue down the corridor.

The last of the gang disappeared around the corner as the procession passed. Again, the hallway went silent, leaving them alone with their thoughts and the hum of the overhead lights.

Dan and Paul exchanged glances, bewildered by the Professor's strange gesture.

"What was that all about?" Paul asked, jerking his thumb toward the hallway. "One minute that guy sounded like he planned to torture us to death slowly, the next he acted like we're at some fancy fencing tournament."

"I think..." Dan hesitated a moment while he thought, "I think he was acknowledging us. I think we've earned his respect or something."

"Great, wonderful," Paul muttered. "The approval of a criminal mastermind. Just what I always wanted. Can't wait to use him as a reference in my business advertising."

"Did you notice how different they all looked?" Dan leaned toward Paul, jerking his head at the corridor. "Like someone let the air out of them."

"Except for Vic," Paul added. "That guy appeared completely unconcerned about the whole thing."

The two sat in quiet for a moment, both drinking their coffee.

Paul put down his cup. "There's one thing I don't get, Danny Boy. Perhaps you can explain it to me."

Dan raised his eyebrows in an unspoken question.

"Mousey." Paul faced Dan. "How he slipped away. You said you nabbed him."

"I did catch him. He just..." Dan shrugged. "I don't know... just wriggled out of my grasp."

"Wriggled out of your grasp?" It was clear Paul didn't believe what Dan was telling him. "But you're older than him. Bigger than him. Stronger than him."

"Yeah, well, you know..." Dan's voice trailed off.

Paul continued to stare.

Dan squirmed. "I mean, Edgar is a nice kid..."

"Edgar? That's his name?"

"Yeah. Norris. Edgar Norris." Dan replied.

"How did you find that out, my dear brother?" Paul leaned back in the chair and crossed his arms. He arched one eyebrow.

"He told me," Dan shot back. "How else do you think I found out, meathead? By checking his birth certificate?"

"You gave the police his name, I suppose." Paul drummed the fingers of one hand on a bicep.

"No, I didn't," Dan fired back. "It... it seemed to have slipped my mind at the time." He took another sip of coffee and paused for a second. "Look, he tied me to that almost rusted-out pipe on purpose. He was trying to help. I mean, he's only a kid and knew he made a mistake. A big one, and he regretted it, and he wanted to change. I remembered Mom and Dad got a second chance, so I figured..."

"You'd let him wriggle out of your grasp," Paul finished.

Dan nodded.

Paul gave his brother an approving nod and an admiring smile. "I get it now."

"You're not going to say anything about him, are you?" Dan asked.

"About whom? I have no idea who you're talking about." Paul put on an innocent expression and picked up his coffee.

Dan grinned and raised his coffee in a toast. "You're the best, buddy."

Paul lifted his cup as well. "Thank you, my dear brother. You're not half-bad yourself. If I must have an identical twin, I'm glad it's you."

"Likewise." The twins tapped their cups together.

"Oh, and Dan, one thing," Paul said. "Please do me a favor."

"Name it, buddy."

Paul leaned toward his brother. "Remember what you did when Betty, Donna and I came to the soda fountain? That fake French accent you used?"

Dan nodded.

Paul pointed a finger at his twin. "Never do it again."

Dan laughed. He crossed his heart. "I promise."

He straightened up, his ears pricking up as he heard footsteps echoing from the hall. There was something distinct about one set of them — sharp and precise, like a metronome. He knew instantly who they belonged to. Sure enough, Mrs. Case, with her usual no-nonsense stride, appeared in the corridor window as she made her way toward the door. Ricardo followed her. Hastily, Dan and Paul scrambled to their feet, their chairs scraping the floor as they got up, a sense of awkwardness lingering in the air.

The conference room door opened, and Ricardo stepped inside with their mother close behind. She greeted each of the twins with a warm hug, then stepped back.

"Are you two okay?" she asked, looking between them.

"We're fine, Mom," Paul answered. Dan nodded in agreement.

"Now then, boys," she said, her voice eerily calm, although her face was a complex map of relief, exhaustion, and simmering irritation. "What on earth —"

She paused when Steve appeared in the hallway and came into the room. Dan and Paul exchanged glances, surprised by the detective's presence, particularly at such a late hour.

Steve stood next to Mrs. Case and grinned at the twins. "Well, Alice, the boys bagged an important one this time."

Dan started, surprised. Why did Steve say "*the* boys" instead of "*your* boys"? The phrase echoed in his mind, stirring a mix of confusion and unease. Was he reading too much into it? He must be, he decided.

"That's true," Ricardo gestured toward the brothers. "These two smashed a huge counterfeiting operation that has stumped us for months. The leader of the group was Andre Jalbert, also known as 'The Professor', because of attending university. He is a French national, infamous for being a master forger and counterfeiter. It's even rumored during the war..."

"He worked with the Germans to create fake British money," Dan said.

Ricardo stopped for a moment, grinned and shook his head. "Of course, you would know that. I'm not going to ask how. Anyway, the Professor was supposed to be involved in Operation Bernhard. That was a Nazi scheme aimed at flooding England and the United States with counterfeit currency to try to crash their economies. After the war, he kept up with his trade, faking money and works of art. With Interpol making things hot, Europe became too risky for him to stay. So he slipped into the US through Canada and set up shop here."

"Jalbert was aiming to become the one-stop for all your counterfeit needs," Steve put in.

Ricardo nodded. "He was printing up thousands of fake bills in different denominations and selling them like a wholesaler all over the country. They even had some overseas customers, so the counterfeits could be used for money laundering."

"But not anymore, thanks to Dan and Paul. The store is closed," Steve added. "And they earned a one-thousand-dollar reward, on top of it."

Dan and Paul grinned at each other and shook hands.

"You should be proud of them, Mrs. Case," Ricardo said. He looked at the twins and beamed with admiration. "They were brilliant. Scattering the counterfeits out of the truck alerted the police. Who thought of that?"

"Chalk that one up to Dan." Paul clapped his brother on the shoulder.

"It was brilliant. I was nearby and heard the officer's radio transmission. I had the squad car turn off after I picked up the tailing of the truck," Ricardo said.

"Were you in the black sedan?" Dan asked.

Ricardo nodded. "From my vehicle, I could organize the raid by radio. You know the rest. We nabbed the gang. Well, most of them."

Dan and Paul exchanged quick glances out of the corners of their eyes.

"The boys must have quite a tale to tell," Steve said.

"They do," Ricardo agreed.

The twins' mother surveyed her two sons with a scrutinizing gaze. With arms crossed, she fixed them with her familiar "now what" look she always had whenever they found themselves caught in mischief.

"Well? Who is going to tell me how you two got involved this time?" she asked.

"You mean how we started on our graduation trip?" Dan began.

"And ended up busting a counterfeit ring?" Paul went on.

"You mean that?" they said together.

Mrs. Case nodded.

The twins pointed at each other. "He will!" they answered as one.